Praise for Joanne Rock

"Any book by Joanne Rock is guaranteed
to be a winner!"
—*CataRomance* on *She Thinks Her Ex Is Sexy...*

"Joanne Rock writes them hot and scorching."
—*Fallen Angel Reviews*

"Hot sex, a spooky mystery, an isolated island
cut off by a storm, ghosts, danger, and
romance—not to mention the perfect ending."
—*Romantic Times BOOKreviews* on *Getting Lucky*

"Grabs you by the throat and
leaves you breathless."
—*Romance Junkies* on *Up Close and Personal*

"For frolicking, sexy fun, Joanne Rock
always delivers!"
—*New York Times* bestselling author Julie Leto

"Sensual stories, sexy heroes and sassy
heroines—fabulous Joanne Rock delivers
keeper-shelf reads!"
—RITA® Award-winning author Catherine Mann

Blaze

Dear Reader,

It's difficult to pinpoint when I first became enamored with sports heroes. From high school football games to college basketball, I always enjoyed whooping it up for the home team. It's a joy that only grew after marrying a pitcher on my college's baseball team—a pitcher who went on to be a sports editor for a variety of newspapers around the country. During those years I had the pleasure of learning about sports from the inside out—the human dramas underlying the plays on the field.

And while my husband was always more interested in the forces that shaped an athlete for greatness, I'll admit I occasionally speculated on a player's love life. What can I say? We were each called to our professions for a reason! I hope you will enjoy the inside peek into four players' romantic journeys during pivotal moments in their careers, in *Sliding into Home.*

It's always a pleasure to hear from readers. You can reach me at joanne@joannerock.com.

Happy reading!

Joanne Rock

Recycling programs
for this product may
not exist in your area.

ISBN-13: 978-0-373-79490-4

SLIDING INTO HOME

www.eHarlequin.com

Printed in U.S.A.

Sliding Into Home

JOANNE ROCK

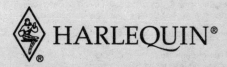

TORONTO • NEW YORK • LONDON
AMSTERDAM • PARIS • SYDNEY • HAMBURG
STOCKHOLM • ATHENS • TOKYO • MILAN • MADRID
PRAGUE • WARSAW • BUDAPEST • AUCKLAND

ABOUT THE AUTHOR

Three-time RITA® Award nominee Joanne Rock turned a passion for writing into a career after imaginary characters kept her awake at night, demanding she tell their stories. The author of more than thirty romances in a variety of subgenres, she has been an avid fan of romance since stumbling upon a Silhouette "First Love" novel as a preteen. After moving around the country for her husband's career, she now calls the gorgeous Adirondack Mountains home—at least until life's next adventure. Learn more about Joanne and her work by visiting her at joannerock.com or myspace.com/joanne_rock.

Books by Joanne Rock

To my three sons, whose athletic prowess is always fun to watch.
And to Dean, the template for each of them.
Thank you for your great genes and for teaching me all about swinging for the fences.

Prologue

"BRODY DAVIS IS AT IT AGAIN, folks." Big Apple Sports Radio disc jockey Brian Marshall launched into his morning topic without prelude as he sat down at a microphone for the drive time show. "Having little tolerance for punks who disrespect the hallowed game of baseball, the Boston Aces' catcher body slammed one of the National League's top players, Chicago Flames' Javier Velasquez in last night's action."

Brian's color commentator was still buttering his bagel and hadn't taken the chair beside him yet, but Brian never needed a lot of help beefing up the sports news. With antics like this to talk about, baseball's stars made his job easy. He settled deeper into his rolling chair behind the blinking red studio light that told the rest of the world he was "on the air."

And on his game. Brian lived for this stuff.

"Velasquez, who hit his league-leading 32nd homer earlier in the game," he continued, warming to the subject, "appeared to boast about his titanic blast while digging in for his second at bat. Davis then called for a high heater, which Boston pitcher Dane Kroc delivered under the chin of Velasquez, who dropped his bat and started toward the mound. Only, Davis would have none of it—he ripped off his mask, grabbed Velasquez, and drove him into the turf, an action sure to draw some sort of suspension."

Ozzie, his color man, was at the ready by now, his bagel dripping butter on the Styrofoam plate as he wheeled his chair closer to his mike.

"The kid definitely needs some grooming from the older players." Ozzie downplayed the story just as Brian had been getting good and revved up. Why did he always have to be Mr. Smooth and Mellow, especially with good dirt like this? "It's the third time this season Davis will get some unwanted time off—once the commissioner's office reviews the tapes—and both he and Velasquez are sure to be fined heavily."

Last night's incident was just one of many this year involving some of the game's most recognized names. And despite the countless replays ESPN was sure to show of Davis's knuckles digging into Velasquez's rib cage, this was not a case where any publicity was good publicity.

But this was the stuff listeners tuned in for.

"So what do you think, Oz? Is baseball in more trouble than usual? We've seen a lot of tabloid-ready escapades from some of the sport's premier players."

Ozzie pressed a button for a track of the seventh inning stretch sound effect to fill some space while he finished chewing, then chimed in.

"At the end of the day, they can drive a ninety-five-mile-per-hour fastball five hundred feet. Or flash some of the finest leather in the league. That's what brings the fans out and in my opinion, that's what will drive the big money contracts at the end of the season."

Geez. Could this guy be any more of a buzz kill?

"We'll see about that, Oz. But since some of today's top defensive players are dominating the headlines, I think we need to talk about 'Gold Gloves' or 'Bold Thugs.' These guys are sure-handed and smooth, rarely dropping the ball on the field, but routinely doing so off it. Listeners, we want to hear what you think."

Oz cracked a grin and shook his head. "So who's on the thug list?"

While the switchboard started lighting up in response to the topic, Brian reeled off a few of the guys they were highlighting to keep the comments focused.

"First up is Brody Davis, one of the brawlers in last night's melee. He was the hope of his franchise last year when the team called him up from the minors. But the moves that dazzled fans in Triple A won't cut it in the majors if Davis can't put a lid on his temper. This is one slugger who might find himself without a contract next spring, even if he manages to capture the fielding recognition his stats deserve."

Oz was juggling calls, but he piped up as he put someone on hold.

"We've already got some votes for our tarnished hometown hero, too." Oz laid in a track of the chant used at the stadium when New York's big hitter came to the plate. "Lance Montero seems to be making the list, but I have to warn our listeners that I don't think being popular with the ladies is the same as being a thug."

Brian tried not to roll his eyes. He was only too glad to put the New York Scrapers' veteran shortstop on the list of sports stars with too much fame and money at their fingertips.

"Montero is practically an institution in the Big Apple, from the South Street Seaport restaurant that bears his name to the guest spots on late-night TV. But Mr. New York could be alienating his fans as he steps out with one famous face after another."

"Although he's hardly the first ballplayer to date a

movie star, you know?" Oz chimed in, taking a pre-dictable long view of the situation.

Brian made a mental note to talk to the guy after today's show. Damn it, they needed to pump up the news with flair and personality, not dull it down to stats and strategy.

"While the public doesn't begrudge a star his en-tourage," Brian continued, pleased to see every line in the studio was already blinking with a call. "Mr. Montero might be pushing the envelope with the long string of women when he's developing a charitable foundation to benefit kids. For all we know, he's setting up a trust fund of sorts for offspring he hasn't publicly acknowl-edged. Don't these guys know that perks like the All-Star Game and the Gold Glove are popularity contests as much as talent?"

"And it looks like there are a couple of calls for Javier Velasquez—"

"Don't get me started!" Brian couldn't believe the talent this kid was pissing away. "The guy has the slug-ging stats and third-base prowess to be a superstar if he didn't spend his free time riding a motorcycle without a helmet and cliff diving around the globe. We all heard there was talk of negotiating a clause into his contract to ensure he stayed healthy, but Velasquez's agent made that disappear. If this guy doesn't rein in his habits, he's another one who'll end up seeing his contract bought out next spring."

"So we've got the fighter, the player, the thrill seeker... at least you've got something besides the steroid scandal to rail about, right, Brian?" Oz chuckled to himself, but Brian was not amused.

They'd nearly come to blows on more than one morning show when he was in the thick of a good tirade about irresponsibility among the players, and

Oz trotted out some crap about the major league cashing in on the new wealth of power hitters and— by turning a blind eye to drug use for years— implying a sort of consent to steroids. Who cared about that? Listeners wanted to talk about the players, not front office people. That stuff was one giant snooze fest.

"How about Mr. Bottom Line, the Atlanta Rebels' Rick Warren?"

"This guy could not play any harder," Oz pointed out, pressing a button that filled the airwaves with the sound of a bat cracking against a ball. "The most over-looked utility player in baseball is up for free agency at the end of the year and I've gotta say I'm rooting for him to land with a team who can make a run at the playoffs."

Surprise, surprise. If baseball had cheerleaders, Oz would be the first one on board.

"This guy's moved around the MLB so often his baseball card collection reads like a travelogue. But after years of showing up ready to play no matter who held his contract, Warren's getting vocal about wanting to be with a club that could give him a shot at the World Series, one of the few destinations he's missed in a long career. He's not winning popularity points by bouncing around so much, is he, Oz?"

Oz mouthed a few choice words, but kept his public commentary to a minimum. "Okay, we're ready for our first caller. Joe, from Queens."

Oz forwarded the caller straight to the air. As he turned off his mic, he muttered something about base-ball being a sport and not a gossip column. But so what? If he had a problem, he'd signed on the wrong show. Brian would be thrilled to see Oz get the boot for his downbeat commentary. For now, however, they settled into their morning routine and continued debating if the boys of summer would hold it together long enough to make the most out of their careers.

FIRED UP

1

Three weeks later

"HAVE YOU BEEN WATCHING the news?"

Feeling like a suspect caught in the act, Naomi Benoit clutched the telephone tighter in one hand as she muted the volume on the television with the other.

"Not since the six o'clock update," she lied to her best friend, forcing her restless feet into her cottage's small kitchen to make a cup of tea. A wicked rainstorm battered the northeast tonight, seemingly centered on Naomi's coastal New Hampshire hometown. Some tea would help ward off the storm's chill and—maybe— help chase off the stupid, misplaced worries tonight's news had stirred up. "And actually, I've got a ton of papers to grade before school tomorrow—"

"Do you believe Brody told the ump to, ah, screw off?"

Shayla had been her best bud since Naomi punched Mugsy Simpson on the playground for lifting Shayla's skirt on a dare. Surely they'd been friends long enough for Shayla to know better than to bring up *him?*

The only ex-boyfriend to ever drag a piece of Naomi's heart along with him when he left. The controversial baseball star Brody Davis.

"Of course he told the ump to go scratch himself." Naomi pulled a shiny red teapot from the cupboard and switched on the burner under her kettle. "Did you see that pitch he called strike three?"

Not that it was any of her concern. How pathetic was it that she would defend a guy who'd ended their relationship via phone while he'd been on the road for a game? He'd never apologized. Never explained. He'd just gotten swept up into baseball and the majors and endorsements for Nike. All of which apparently ranked higher than his hometown girlfriend on his personal radar.

Still, her gaze strayed to ESPN's replay of today's home plate shouting match in spite of herself.

"It looked low to me." Shayla sighed on the other end of the phone. "But why can't he ever walk away? Doesn't he realize they'll never renew his contract, let alone consider him for the Gold Glove he deserves? I keep thinking Brody will get past the big outbursts one of these days, but—"

"Did I mention I had papers to grade?" Naomi's heart shouldn't twist over a conversation about an afternoon Boston Aces game at the home field just two hours south of them. She and Shay had been fans of the team since the sixth grade when Boston traded some upstart pitching prospect for Lyle Daringer, the hottest slugger on the planet at that time. But with Brody a fixture on the Aces' roster this year, Naomi found she couldn't dish about the games quite as much as in the old days.

Although, in her defense, she'd dated with a vengeance after the breakup to oust Brody from her heart. She thought she'd done a damn good job of it, too, until her most recent ex-boyfriend suggested she was only interested in baseball because she carried a torch for her first love.

As if.

"Can you hear the subtle nuances of my cold silence

on this end of the phone?" Shayla asked, remaining quiet for all of two seconds to illustrate her point. "Who am I going to talk baseball with if you find something else to do every time Brody's name comes up?"

Naomi's cat, Zora, twined around her legs and meowed, recognizing Naomi's proximity to the cat treat cabinet. She pulled out the container like any well-trained pet owner and sprinkled a snack in Zora's bowl.

"You can hear Mike and Tony battle it out on *Pardon the Interruption* if you want some insights. At least they won't write off his beef the way that snarky DJ on Big Apple Sports Radio will. Because while Brody might be the type to dump his girlfriend in the most tacky manner possible, he sure as heck wouldn't argue a strike call without damn good reason." She could respect the guy's prowess on the diamond without carrying a freaking torch for him.

And frankly, as a die-hard Aces fan, Naomi hated the flap Brody's antics had caused in baseball circles, taking focus off the game and putting it on his...*colorful* character. She didn't know what was up with him, but he was having a hell of a rookie year. The stats were amazing, but he seemed to touch off controversy at every other game.

"One last question," Shayla pushed, stretching Naomi's patience as the kettle began to whistle. "Do you think they'll try to trade him for this?"

The hiss of steam blared through the kitchen, almost drowning out the roll of pounding thunder. Naomi tugged her sweater tighter around her and lifted the pot to fill her teacup. As the whistling ceased, she realized the pounding wasn't thunder.

Bam, bam, bam!

It was a knock at her door.

"Someone's here. I'll see you in school tomorrow,

okay?" Setting down the phone and the kettle, she hurried to the front door, wondering who would brave the storm. Zora kept pace, planting her furry cat body wherever she was about to step, nearly tripping her twice before she reached the door.

She pulled it open to see the same face that had filled her TV screen in highlight reels ever since the one o'clock game in Boston.

Dripping rain and testosterone, hometown hero Brody Davis stood on her porch step.

"TEN MINUTES." BRODY FIGURED he'd better start small in his requests if he wanted to gain admittance to Naomi's house after a year of silence. A year of knowing he'd thrown away the best shot he'd ever had at real happiness. "That's all I'm asking. Can I talk to you for ten minutes?"

Frowning, she studied him while the wind whipped his baseball jacket, the gusts driving the pelting rain on his back. She held the door open wide enough that the elements blew around the magazines and papers on a coffee table just behind her, but she seemed oblivious to the tempest. She appeared more concerned with how to tell him off while he stood before her—a wet hat literally in hand—ready to talk.

And more.

"C'mon, Naomi," he urged, miserable from the inside out. "I already struck out once tonight. You can't ring me up a second time."

Just remembering the fight with the ump and the ensuing dress down from his manager torqued him off all over again. But the mention of his latest outburst drew a lopsided grin from his former girlfriend.

Damn, but she was hot. Not manicured, groomed perfection. But real-woman sexy. Her fiery-red hair and take-no-crap attitude had turned his head at a young age and set the standard for what he would find appealing in a woman for the rest of his life. Still, though they'd dated on and off in high school, they hadn't really gotten serious until last year when he'd been on a farm team close to town.

"I can pretty much guarantee you won't be scoring in this house, Slugger," she drawled, standing aside to let him enter. "But I've got ten minutes if you'd like to dry off before I send you back down the highway to Boston in that jaunty little sports car."

Amen.

She could pick on his ride all she wanted. She didn't know he'd already scored a victory tonight. Just stepping into Naomi Benoit's house was like coming home. A unique feeling for a scrappy kid whose teenage parents had passed him around to every relative they could scrounge in an effort to abdicate his upbringing.

Finding Naomi tonight had been his overriding goal from the moment he'd walked out of the Aces' clubhouse in the wake of the great meltdown. He wanted her back. And he'd been waiting for her to be free for the past six months. Lucky for Brody, he still had enough friends in town to keep tabs on her so he could jump into the fray the moment he'd heard she had split with her boyfriend. He wasn't taking any chances she'd find someone new after she broke up with the latest guy.

"Thank you." He stood on the front mat and took the door out of her hands since she didn't seem inclined to close it. Shutting it behind him, he absorbed the sights and sounds of Naomi and her world. "Great place you've got here."

He knew she couldn't abide small talk, but it was his

first reaction that was safe to utter since he couldn't possibly tell her she looked good enough to devour.

When they'd broken up, she'd been house shopping. Her apartment had been tiny and they'd both been ready for more room, but he hadn't been around to help her make the move. But his eye was taken by her and not the digs. She was a gorgeous redhead whose tomboy ways were masked beneath eclectic clothes with girly touches. Even tonight, roaming her living room in navy-striped pajama pants and a Boston Aces T-shirt, she sported a jeweled double headband that kept her wavy auburn hair off her face. The headband had a purple butterfly perched over one ear.

She clutched a mug in one hand and her house smelled like scented candles and flavored tea. Something cinnamony. Something sexy. Of course, sex had never been far from his mind when Naomi was around, one of many reasons he'd thought they should take a break a year ago. He'd wanted to focus on his career.

"Oh, please." Naomi set down the mug and disappeared into a back room for a second before returning with a blue bath towel. She threw it at him before plunking into a green paisley wingback across from a fireplace with a single burning log. "You're living in something that looks like the Playboy mansion and you think *this* place is nice?" She shook her head. "I'm not buying it. Why don't you have a seat and tell me what you really came here for."

Scrubbing the towel across his short hair, Brody finished drying off and slipped out of his shoes before leaving the front mat. He dropped the towel next to his loafers, thinking how much the whitewashed New England cottage stuffed with quirky furnishings suited her.

"My house is 6,500 square feet of vacant floor space

and baseball memorabilia. It's about as welcoming as a sporting good store." Not ready to spill his real reason for seeking her out yet, he hoped to distract her. "Any chance of snagging some tea, or is that pushing my luck?"

He flexed his sore hands, thinking it might help to wrap them around a mug. His trainer had told him to ice the knuckles he'd scraped up after putting his fist through his locker, but Brody couldn't stand the idea of being any colder.

"The water's hot." She nodded toward a tiny galley kitchen with a stove that looked like it came from the 1930s and a bright red teapot on the white tile countertop beside it. "Help your— What happened to your hands?"

She set her cup down on the coffee table made of a lacquered tree stump just as he stood up. Darting past her, he snatched the teapot and rummaged around her cabinets until he found a second cup.

"It's not a big deal." Of course, it was a big deal to let his temper get the best of him for the umpteenth time this season, but the cuts on his hands were the least of his worries.

She snatched up his right arm before he could grab a mug. He hadn't been prepared for how her touch would affect him. Purple-painted fingernails barely grazed his skin, the pinkies graced with tiny daisies. A silver Celtic bangle wound around her wrist, a gift from her parents on her sixteenth birthday. He vaguely remembered her friend hosting a big bonfire party to mark the date.

Now, the fruity scent of her shampoo tempted him to lean closer, and he realized she'd just showered. A few damp strands of hair remained darker than the rest and her skin had been scrubbed clean of any makeup. A shot of pure longing jolted his insides as he remembered showers together. Whole days spent in bed…

"Please tell me you used the fist on an inanimate object?" Her chin tipped up as she met his gaze and she let go of his hand in a hurry.

Had his carnal thoughts been that obvious?

"Of course." He poured hot water in his mug while she slid him a tea bag. "You know me better than that."

"I thought I did until you went after Javier Velasquez the last time you played Chicago." She shot him an assessing look for a moment before she reached into the freezer for a package of frozen vegetables and passed it to him. "You should hold that on your hand."

"It was a tense game and he was talking smack." Still, he'd never lost it like that before. His world had been falling apart ever since his breakup with Naomi and he didn't know why. He'd thought it would be a good idea to focus on his career. But lately everything he touched went up in flames. "And you should know that Velasquez was cool about it afterward. He plays the way I do, you know? He doesn't leave anything on the field. It's the media that blew it out of proportion."

Taking the tea and the green beans, he stalked out of the kitchen to take a seat on her couch.

"I never thought you would piss away your shot at the majors." She followed more slowly, studying him over the rim of her mug. "I couldn't believe you were ripping into that ump on national TV after you've been warned to keep a rein on your tendency to, shall we say, speak your mind?"

He knew he shouldn't be flattered she'd kept tabs on his career. She'd been a baseball enthusiast, and particularly an Aces fan, since long before they'd dated. Still, it pleased him to know she hadn't carried a big enough grudge against him to make her root for New York.

"Did you see that strike-three call?"

The Aces had been down by a run in the eighth when he'd come up to bat. There were two outs with runners on second and third and Brody had two legitimate strikes on him for multiple balls he'd fouled off trying to work the count. As a catcher, he'd sat behind home plate all game and he knew the ump's strike zone. The guy had been calling the outside corner all day for both pitchers, squeezing them hard. But it had started to rain sometime in the seventh and maybe the guy didn't want to stick around for extra innings with bad weather on the way. When the next pitch came, it was low and outside, same as a hundred other balls that afternoon.

Brody had let that one past him, confident as hell about the placement, yet the home plate ump had given the strike-three sign and ended the game.

"Yes. And it was a bad call. But you and I both know that's not the first one and it won't be the last. There's no instant replay in baseball. The umps call the game like they see it."

He chugged the tea, hoping to ingest some calm even if he scalded his tongue in the process. Fortunately, just sitting in Naomi's living room brought his blood pressure down a few notches. Funny how she could tell him the same damn thing his manager had three hours ago and it didn't make him want to put his fist through anything.

"Sometimes arguing convinces the ump to make the next call in your team's favor," he insisted, knowing for a fact that was true. "We've seen that happen."

"Right. But this isn't stickball in the backyard with Shayla's big brother umping the game. This is the big leagues and the manager decides what to dispute. He doesn't get paid a million per year to let you do his job for him—and a sloppy one at that."

Every word she said made total sense. He'd known all

of it before he'd showed up here. But somehow hearing her say it helped. She'd always had a practical fairness that appealed to him. She could cut through his B.S. faster than any female he'd ever met and some perverse part of him had wondered if she still held that power.

Sure enough, the woman was still more potent than the homemade rotgut his granddad once brewed on a falling-down farm not ten miles up the road from Naomi's cottage.

"You're right," he acknowledged, polishing off the tea and setting aside the frozen veggies.

"You can't honestly expect me to believe you drove here in a thunderstorm after we haven't spoken in a year because you wanted my input on a bad call." She punched a button on the remote to turn off the television just as a highlight from his earlier argument flashed on the screen.

She hadn't moved fast enough to erase that unflattering image of himself—red faced and tense—from his head.

"No." Jolting to his feet, he roamed around the small living area in his socks, restless with too much tension. "It's complicated."

Her silver bracelet clanked against her mug as she gripped it more tightly. Thunder rolled outside, the rain pummeling the roof.

"I'm a smart woman. Try me."

"Nothing's been the same since you—since we—" He didn't know where to begin. "I always felt more grounded when I lived up here. When we were dating."

Frowning, she set the remote on the coffee table and remained silent. Waiting.

"That much is fact. What I don't understand is why

or what variable in my life I need to adjust to fix it." It was like trying to iron out a hitch in your swing. You went back to basics to sort out the trouble.

"And you think *I* could be a variable?" Her nose wrinkled with confusion or maybe distaste.

"I need to figure out why I can't settle down in the box. Why I can't sit still in a hotel room when we're on the road for games. Why I'm restless as hell all the time, even when I'm knocking the ball out of the park." He'd circled her floor multiple times and forced himself to stop.

To face her.

"I'm confused." She shook her head, clearly having no idea where he was going with this.

"Maybe I lost some mojo when we broke up." It sounded stupid. It *was* stupid. But after telling himself that was the dumbest thing he'd ever come up with and having the damn idea persist, he figured he owed it to himself to test the theory.

He was better with her than without her and the time had come to reclaim the woman who'd become a part of him.

"Brody." She straightened in her chair. "You made it through the ranks of the minors and into the majors. You've got a multi-million-dollar contract. You've dated the chicks in the *SI* swimsuit issue. Trust me, your mojo is formidable."

"Yeah?" He stalked across the living room and dropped down to sit on her coffee table inches from where she sat. "I think I never got over you."

Her blue eyes widened. A slight flush crawled across her skin. He was close enough to see her pulse throb at the base of her throat.

"You can't be suggesting—"

His hand on her knee halted whatever she'd been

about to say and he remembered every single time he'd ever touched her. Every single time they'd taken their attraction to a heart-pounding, mind-numbing conclusion.

"Give me another chance, Naomi."

2

"YOU'RE CERTIFIABLE."

Naomi's heart fluttered like she was sixteen again and she cursed the breathlessness he inspired. He'd been the one to leave her behind while he chased his super-star dreams. She'd coped by becoming a serial dater, making sure she never stuck around long enough to get her heart broken again. The method hadn't helped her find true love, but she was managing to have some fun in the process.

There was no way he could coerce her into—what? Sex? A relationship? Because he'd lost his *mojo*.

"Tell me something I don't know." He stared at her with heart-melting gray eyes, his good looks sharper and more defined since high school. He'd filled out in the last six years, his body honed into a slugging machine. He had the upper body strength of a power hitter and rock-hard catcher's thighs. Not that she was ogling him now, but she might have ogled a time or two on television.

In fact, there were probably an embarrassing number of interviews with him recorded on her DVR, although they were strictly used for the sake of the inspirational videos she put together for the youth baseball team she coached. Surreptitiously, she hid the remote control between the seat cushions.

"So you don't care that you're barking mad?" She

reached to tuck a stray hair into her headband and realized her fingers felt a little trembly.

Heaven help her, Brody Davis was getting under her skin again and he'd been back in her life for all of ten minutes. And that ticked her off.

"When have I ever cared what anyone else thinks?" he asked in all seriousness, his chiseled features set in stark lines.

She spied a darkness in his gaze that he'd never revealed in any of his interviews.

"You're serious." It wasn't until that moment that the full import of why he'd shown up really hit her.

He'd honestly come here to get back together with her.

Or maybe just to spend a night in her bed.

And he wasn't here so she could be some notch on an already-impressive bedpost—her notch had been left a long time ago. He really thought sleeping with her would straighten out whatever problems were chasing around his head tonight.

"Like a heart attack." His words whispered over her with deafening softness, uttered by a man she'd let get too close.

In more ways than one.

"No way—"

He flexed his fingers against her pj-clad knee, reminding her that he'd been touching her that whole time and she hadn't done jack to stop him. That big, broad, powerful palm that halted hundred-mile-an-hour fastballs day in and day out, now touched her with infinite gentleness. Heat.

"Naomi." The word was a plea. Or maybe a chastisement. She couldn't tell because she was too caught up in the feel of his touch and the intoxication of having him this close.

She tried hard to call up the way it had felt when he'd broken up with her long distance and followed it up with a rambling e-mail at one in the morning to explain they'd both be "better off."

A little of the anger came back—slowly. She let it build, knowing her righteous indignation was tempered by the subtle stroke of his thumb on the underside of her knee as the rain thundered against the windows, sealing them in this moment.

"You hurt me too much to deserve that opportunity," she admitted finally, needing to say the words out loud so her hormones got the message.

"So you can hurt me in return," he suggested, sliding forward on the coffee table so that his knees bracketed hers and his hand glided up her thigh three breath-stealing inches. "Tomorrow, you can kick me out and send me back to Boston a spurned man. But consider just this one night…"

She wanted to flip his hand off her leg—the touch was nervy for a man who hadn't seen her in months. In fact, she wanted to flip him off, period. But no matter how much she tried to tell herself otherwise, she'd never fully excised Brody Davis from her heart. Besides, the dark, haunted look in his eyes gave her pause.

She could still read his moods like an old farmer read the weather. She'd known he'd tell off that ump tonight the second she'd seen his jaw clench. And she knew right now that he wasn't spinning some lover-boy nonsense to get in her bed. He was as intense in a relationship as he was on the field. The man was far from shallow.

He had to be genuinely worried about losing his career because of his outbursts and he'd come to her for—what? To help keep him grounded? To level out one of his legendary moods?

"Sleeping with me won't fix whatever you think has gone wrong for you." Her gaze tracked over his face, searching for more clues to this confusing and complex man who'd charmed her from the moment he'd whispered an answer to her in Spanish class.

Not that she'd needed help, sitting in an accelerated program with kids one and two years ahead of her. But Brody had wanted to talk to her and found a way, even though the answer he'd given her had been wrong.

"If you're right, then I'll be the one who has to deal with it." He didn't appear overly concerned.

Of course, he'd had total confidence in his incorrect Spanish answer, too. Naomi had always admired his ability to ignore obstacles and plow ahead in life. Right or wrong, he'd achieved so much simply by brazening his way through the world.

"What if I had a boyfriend or a husband?"

He smiled for the first time since he'd stepped back into her life.

"I've been keeping tabs on you, too." He reached to tuck that loose strand of hair into her headband, his other hand never leaving her thigh. "You're still teaching and coaching youth softball. You've been dating, but there haven't been any serious boyfriends besides the X-Games dude you told to take a hike a couple of weeks ago."

She couldn't believe he'd kept track, right down to her recent breakup. "The X-Games guy is actually an environmental engineer." Her cheek tingled where he'd brushed away the stray strands.

"Whatever." He rolled his eyes, unimpressed. "So he's a hardcore granola eater. I watched his dirt bike routine one night to see what all the hype was about and I figured he'd break his neck by the time he's thirty, then where would that leave you?"

He sounded protective, possessive and far too jealous for a guy whose dating life got press in newspapers, magazines and—for the really addicted sports fan—online. Nevertheless, she'd broken up with the X-Gamer for precisely the reasons he mentioned.

Of course, the X-Gamer hadn't taken it so well. Ryan had quickly made it known that she hadn't been breaking up with him because of what he *did,* but because he *wasn't* Brody. Naomi had been furious. But she would have to find a way to get along with him eventually since he coached one of the other softball teams in her league. They had to see each other every weekend.

"Okay. I didn't mean to suggest my private life was up for discussion. Clearly, you've got access to better research than I gave you credit for." Someone from their hometown must be keeping him up-to-date on what she'd been doing. Naomi took small comfort in that since it meant she wasn't the only one to seek out information on an ex.

Him.

Heaven knew, she'd never tried to find out what Ryan was doing in the short time since they'd split. Maybe that was because their relationship had run a more natural course, whereas she and Brody had broken up prematurely. Over the freaking telephone.

And what if there was a certain messed-up logic in Brody's idea that they should have sex? Would it have helped cure her of Brody if things hadn't ended so abruptly? If their relationship had died a more natural death?

"You're free of emotional entanglements right now, and so am I." He sat very still, not pressing his luck with the hand on her thigh, but not retreating, either. "Don't you ever think about me? About what it would have been like if we'd stayed together?"

A lie sat on her tongue, all ready for automatic discharge. But just then, a flash of lightning brought a clap of thunder so loud the windowpanes rattled in the casements. She remembered the old childhood vow about "may I be struck dead" for lying and thought maybe she shouldn't test the issue with lightning dancing all around the house.

"Sometimes. Maybe." She shivered at the thought. Memories of endless kisses on the bench seat of his old pickup truck returned with sizzling clarity.

Ryan had accused her of being hung up on Brody and she'd denied it to him the same way she so often denied it to herself. But since she hadn't managed a solid relationship with any of the guys she'd dated since the man in front of her, maybe it wouldn't be such a bad idea to prove in no uncertain terms that she could put Brody in her past. She could sleep with him, see that sex with him wasn't the monumental experience her brain had built it up to be, and walk away from him for good.

It had been his idea, after all. He would hardly be surprised if she sent him packing in the morning.

"I've thought about it, too," he admitted, his striped dress shirt open over a gray T-shirt that followed the lines of his perfectly maintained bod. "A lot. Too much lately."

"Belated guilt?" she guessed, thinking about what it would be like to forget their shared past and launch herself into the arms of her fantasy man. No way could he live up to her memories of him. All the better for shuttling him out of her memory so she could get on with her life. "Better late than never, I guess."

All thought of sending him away tonight was fading. Maybe it had been a moot point since the moment she'd opened her door. Something about his presence in her living room—asking for a replay of the past—felt inevitable. Destined.

"It's not guilt that made me drive two hours in a downpour." His gaze shifted south to linger on her mouth. "I couldn't see the road half the time."

"You're too reckless by half," she accused, her tongue darting along her suddenly dry lips.

Now that she'd given herself permission to be with him just this once, her body was responding with enthusiasm.

"There was a time you had a bit of a reckless streak yourself." He twined a hand behind her neck and she was lost.

She wasn't sure how she'd feel in the morning when Brody was excised from her life forever. But by her calculation, she had a good seven hours before she needed to worry about it.

"I think you bring out the brash side of me." The man was an electric spark. He jolted everyone and everything around him.

And, tomorrow morning aside, Naomi couldn't wait for her dose of sizzle.

SHE WAS GOING TO LET HIM STAY.

Brody read it in her eyes the second before he kissed her, and the magnitude of that gift hit him like a fastball to the chest. His heart damn near stopped.

Thankfully, the forward momentum of his mouth never slowed.

Her lips met his in a slow dance he hadn't forgotten. This was *Naomi*. His girl. The One Who Got Away—but only because he'd let her go.

Shutting down the old thoughts before they stole tonight from him, too, Brody forgot everything else but kissing her. Fingers tunneling through her hair, he freed the jeweled headband to slip to the floor, welcoming the silken slide of the strands on his skin. He angled her head, deepening the kiss, giving her as much as she asked for. More.

Her hands roamed his back, her touch even more potent than he remembered. She traced the muscles he'd fought for in daily training sessions, her fingers missing nothing in their thorough tour of his upper body.

He drew her closer, lifting her up off the couch to sit on his lap, cradling her against him. She fit him perfectly, all lean curves and sleek limbs as she wound herself around him. Seeking even more contact.

But then, Naomi had never been the kind of person to doubt herself once she made a decision. She gave a hundred and ten percent to whatever she chose in life and—for tonight at least—she'd chosen him. Making no attempt to hide her hunger, she splayed a hand across his chest and slid it around his shoulder, sealing herself to him.

His control slipped a bit more and he pulled her hips tight to his. Their kiss heated, their tongues battling out an old score their bodies would settle once and for all.

"Do you need a bed?" No one had ever accused him of any great finesse with women, and he regretted the harsh sound of the words as they croaked from his throat.

For all of a second and a half.

Naomi's eyes were unfocused and desire-filled as she stared up at him and frowned.

"Hell, no." She traced his lower lip with her finger. "A bed is at least twenty feet away and I'm not giving you any chance to change your mind."

He might have smiled, but the need to put his mouth back on hers was so fierce, he didn't have time to.

Outside, the rain escalated to impossible volume, drowning out any other sounds. The primal, driving force of it echoed everything inside him, his relentless need for the woman in his arms.

Spearing a hand beneath her shirt, he covered the creamy skin with questing fingers. He made quick work of the hooks on her bra, a smooth expanse of satin that he pulled off along with her shirt.

Breaking the kiss, he had to see her, to revere what he'd unveiled. She was as curvy as he remembered, her breasts generous for her small frame. The taut pink crests were rosy and slightly upturned, awaiting his mouth. Gladly, he obliged.

Tilting her back, he supported her with one arm and cupped the soft weight of her breast with his free hand. He kneaded her warm flesh, watching the way her eyes slid to half-mast, her breathing growing frantic.

Lowering his lips to one tight peak, he circled the tip with his tongue, drawing out the moment before he drew her deep in his mouth to suckle her. Not even the rain could smother her cry as he lavished kisses there.

Not content to savor her with his mouth alone, he trailed a hand down her stomach to the waistband of her thin cotton pajama pants. Unfastening the drawstring, he freed the waist, but didn't penetrate the barrier yet, preferring to linger over the heat of her skin and the feel of her in his arms. He dipped a finger into the small depression of her belly button and she arched hard, calling out his name.

And then, playtime was over.

Naomi twisted his shirt in her hand, gripping the fabric tight to drag one layer and then the other up his shoulders and off. She slipped free from his grasp when he moved to help her, her pajama pants sliding to the floor to reveal a hot-pink thong with a rhinestone star on each hip. His hands were on her instantly, framing her waist, but she still wasn't done with him. Her fingers plucked at his belt buckle, wrenching leather this way and that until she'd unfastened the belt, button and zipper in record time.

A flash of lightning crackled again, its appearance coinciding with a soft *pop* and the loss of electricity. The lamps faded to black, casting the room in darkness save for the bursts of lightning that provided a strobe effect.

If Naomi was concerned about the power outage, she sure didn't show it. Her fingers never wavered from a slow track down his abs to the waistband of his shorts.

"Damn," she whispered softly, leaning to press a kiss on his chest, her tongue darting out to trace a teasing circle just above his heart.

"What?" He didn't want to interrupt what was happening between them, but for her he'd fix anything and everything that ticked her off.

"I didn't get to see the best part," she confided, her fingers slipping into his shorts to stroke the hard length of him.

"I think I could have fixed that problem if you'd waited to touch me." Heat seared his skin, flaying his insides and torching all rational thought. "Now, I can't do anything but this."

He picked her up and held her against his chest, positioning the vee of her thighs to press against the tip of his erection. Lights flashed behind his eyes that didn't have a damn thing to do with the storm. Naomi's arms wrapped around him, clinging. Her breasts swelled against his chest.

His heartbeat kicked into overdrive, the thumping louder than a stadium full of fans at fever pitch. Anchoring her against him, he tugged down her panties with one hand until they slid to the floor.

Later, he would touch her. Taste her. Pile on so many orgasms she wouldn't see any man but him for the next decade. Or ten.

But right now, he needed to be inside her. Laying her down on the sofa, he shed his shorts and felt around for his pants on the floor until he found the right pocket. He withdrew a condom and rolled it on, heedless of her hands tugging him down to the couch.

To her.

If he didn't sheathe himself now, it wasn't going to happen. It had been far too long since he'd touched her.

Positioning himself over her, he parted her thighs and allowed himself just one feel. Circling the hot center of her, his finger slid easily along the swollen folds. Her wordless plea assured him she was ready and he entered her in one breathless stroke.

Possessing her.

He felt the surge to his core, just the way he knew he would have every day for the last year if he hadn't made a colossal mistake. Words of praise and commitment, reverence and—ah, hell—more than that bubbled in his throat.

Ruthlessly, he held it all back, determined to give her one night that wasn't about anything else but pleasure.

She wrapped her legs around him, her slender thighs squeezing, locking. She arched her hips, meeting every stroke, taking all he had to give. He framed her face in his hands and kissed her, mirroring the slow glide of his hips with his tongue.

Heat blazed over his back, dotting his shoulders with sweat as he kept his movements seductively easy. Gentle. He could feel her tension mounting around him as she stilled, her breasts heaving with gusty breaths punctuated with little moans.

Just when she turned the most rigid, her fingers digging into his shoulders, he increased his pace. A cry wrenched from her lips. She writhed beneath him, so gorgeous in her pleasure, her muscles clenching his tight. He let go then, losing himself in the lush feel of her and the absolute perfection of the moment.

Later, he wrapped her tight in his arms, side by side on the couch. His heart slammed hard against his ribs for a long time afterward, as if it wanted to make itself known.

After all, he hadn't just come here for one night with Naomi, no matter what he'd allowed her to think.

3

NAOMI'S ALARM WENT OFF, the wailing electronic beep ruining the great dream she'd been having about Brody...

Oh, wait. It hadn't been a dream this time. She felt the very real proof wrapped around her, spooned against her in the tangle of sheets. The alarm hadn't ended a great dream. It had ended her brief reunion with Brody, a one-night indulgence that had been far too delectable for words. Being with Brody had been...transporting. Amazing.

And oh, man, she was in over her head.

"You can't seriously be thinking of getting out of bed at this hour." Brody's hand shifted where it lay on her hip, skating along the indentation of her waist and dipping lower to tease a response from her body that awakened it instantly.

"I coach kids' softball on Saturday mornings, remember? I have no choice."

Of course, she'd set the alarm early, after the power came back on, so she'd have time to say goodbye. Time for her heart to recover from her night with a man she'd always cared about more than she could admit. And their night together hadn't done a damn thing to lessen the attraction.

The caring.

Her heart tightened in her chest. The parting was not going to be easy.

"Naomi." He softened his tone and twisted her around in his arms so they faced each other.

Dawn hadn't fully broken yet, so his expression remained shadowed. She hoped hers did, too, since she feared giving away the feelings last night had stirred.

"Mmm?"

"Breaking up with you was the hardest thing I've ever done."

Surprised but wary, she squinted through the dimness to meet his steely gaze. She had not expected to have this kind of conversation. Nor did she want to remember the aftermath of their breakup.

"I assume that's why you opted out of splitting with me in person and chose to simply dial my digits while you were a thousand miles away." The sheets cooled at the thought and she was grateful she'd left ample time before she needed to shower and be at the practice field.

She sent up a prayer of thanksgiving that the rain had stopped during the night. She needed that field to be dry enough to play on by 8:00 a.m. because she needed something to get her mind off Brody.

"I was a chicken shit and I hated myself for it, but I swear to you, I would not have been able to look you in the eye and tell you it was over when I still loved you like crazy." His gaze never wavered, as if he spouted the God's honest truth when she knew he was full of it.

Suddenly, the prospect of walking away from him this morning seemed a little easier.

"Don't you dare lie to me after what we just shared—"

"How many times did people tell us how tough it would be to make a relationship work while I was on the road and you were here?"

"And you decided to buy into the naysayers' logic without telling me? After all the plans we'd made for a future together?" She regretted the note of outrage in her voice that hinted at how much he'd hurt her. What happened to using their night together to get him out of her head for good?

"I was going to spring training in Florida and then 162 games around the country while you were committed to a job here. How fair would it have been to ask you to wait for me while I traveled around the country with a major league team? How many relationships do you know that could have survived that?"

"Why didn't you tell me that instead of giving me the heave-ho like I was some girl you picked up in a bar?" She was shaking with the memory of it even now. Or maybe she was shaking because he'd made her feel something incredible last night and then brought up all this garbage first thing this morning.

Why couldn't they have parted civilly, with the taste of kisses on their lips, instead of angry words? But then, Brody always had a way of sweeping you into his world, firing you up and making you feel as passionate as he did. Good or bad, his emotions were contagious.

"I was too conflicted about the whole thing to have broken up with you if I hadn't had your anger to seal the deal. I knew in my heart it was wrong to drag you out on the road with me when you were excited to buy a house and put down roots." He ignored her spluttered protest and pressed a finger to her lips. "Besides, we'd hardly dated anyone but each other. I had this idea in my head that you should date other people so you wouldn't resent me for monopolizing most of your romantic life."

She wanted to argue about how unfair it had been

to deceive her. About how wrong he'd been to make a big relationship decision without her, and to break her heart because he thought he knew what was best for her. But something—maybe the sincerity she saw in his eyes as the sunlight filtered through the blinds—made her think twice.

He'd been under a lot of pressure when he signed with the Aces. And his family had all been there with their hands out when they heard about his fat contract. As exciting as his career had been, it had shown him who his real friends were.

Too bad that—after finding out—he'd turned his back on her, too.

"So instead of resenting you for tying me down, you made me resent you for ditching me without so much as a face-to-face conversation."

He shook his head. "I never suggested it was a well thought out plan. If you haven't noticed, I've got a habit of occasionally putting my foot in my mouth."

In the quiet moment that followed his response, she remembered the way he'd started the conversation. The bit about loving her so much he couldn't have broken up with her in person. Why had he brought that up this morning when her emotions were so mixed up to start with?

Unwilling and possibly unable to see straight where he was concerned, Naomi couldn't think about it right now. Not with the scent of him on her sheets and her skin.

"I'd better get dressed." She scrambled out of bed before he could stop her, too confused to continue a conversation that shredded her insides. "I don't want to keep the kids waiting. They've got a big game this week and really need the practice, so—"

She hightailed toward the bathroom, needing a retreat.

"I'm coming with you," he called, his sexy, he-man

voice easily penetrating the bathroom door. "I want to see you in action. Besides, I don't know if I've got a job to show up for today anyhow."

Flipping on the handle for the shower, Naomi made a valiant effort to drown out the noisy hubbub of her feelings. She told herself Brody only wanted to hang out with her today because he might have been released from his contract after the fight with the ump and the manager yesterday. He'd showed up here last night because he'd been upset and for all she knew, that was the only thing keeping him in New Hampshire when the rest of his life was in Boston.

Too bad no matter how much she scrubbed and rinsed, the voice in her head kept insisting there was a chance he had come back to his hometown for more than a respite from the media storm. After the amazing time they'd had together last night, a little part of her wanted to believe Brody had another reason for coming home: her.

NAOMI WAS A HELL OF A COACH.

Brody realized as much within the first fifteen minutes of her softball practice for eleven- and twelve-year-olds. He'd never had time to be in town during one of her practices before, something he realized now had been a sign of how scattered his attention had been during the months they'd dated.

He hadn't been surprised by her adeptness since she'd always had a sharp eye for sports. Plus, she could motivate anyone. Witness the way she'd encouraged him to follow a dream—starting way back in high school—that would have been easy to give up on so many times. No wonder the kids on the soggy field listened when she spoke and worked their hardest to gain her approval.

He'd laid low while the parents had dropped off the kids, figuring he'd save the mob scene for later. The kids thought it was cool a baseball player had come to help them out with a practice—but not so cool that they didn't return to flicking one another's hats off or giggling about a sleepover they'd attended the week before.

Brody had talked Naomi into giving him a lift since the two-seater convertible he'd been tooling around in lately was on the conspicuous side. Mostly, he just wanted more time to be with her and convince her to give him a second chance. His approach this morning had resulted in a stalemate, making him think he'd screwed up too badly last year for her to reconsider where he was concerned.

"Heads up, Jess," Naomi warned, shouting to the shortstop on one of her scrimmage teams after she'd split the group in two for game-style practice.

A tall girl was in the box, waiting for her pitch and the shortstop tensed, eye on the batter. Brody had been watching the in-fielder during the warm-up drills and the kid was good for her age—athletic, coordinated, quick thinking.

She was ready to make a play, knees bent, poised on the balls of her feet. From Naomi's heads-up to the shortstop, Brody guessed that's where the batter normally hit the ball. Another sign of good coaching— Naomi paid attention to the finer points of the game and kept her team on their toes.

When the batter cracked a fastball, she hit a line drive right at the shortstop's head. It would have been a tough play for anyone at that level, requiring quick thinking and deft reflexes. In fact, Brody figured the fielder would be damn fortunate just not to get hit. Instead, Jess made a beautiful, textbook-style backhand stab at the ball.

And missed it.

"Damn it!" Jess kicked the ground with a vengeance, the display of temper effectively halting the other team's celebration as the runner passed first and sped toward second.

Brody felt the fielder's pain like he'd bet no one else on the diamond did. The few parents who'd stuck around to watch the practice appeared vaguely horrified that their eleven-year-olds were subject to the tantrum. The language that would have been mild on a professional field was surely off-limits for a grade-school team.

For some reason, seeing the shortstop's face twisted up in a snarl of anger—at herself, not at the batter—gave Brody a better look in the mirror than watching professional athletes lose their cool. That was how he'd looked to fifty thousand fans at the Aces ballpark yesterday. This was how he'd appeared on the jumbotron and on TV screens in a few million homes.

Like a temperamental kid who couldn't keep his cool.

Naomi blew the whistle and called the teams in for a water break as she hurried over to the infield grass. Jess had thrown her glove on second base, clearly still pissed she'd missed a ball and not terribly wise to the upset she'd caused all around. Brody followed her, not to nose his way into her business, but because he didn't like the idea of her talking to any ticked off person alone, even one who was eleven years old.

"Hey, Jess." She picked up the glove and handed it back to the player. "Tough break on the play, but let's give credit where it's due, okay? Tyra had an awesome hit. That kind of bat speed keeps us competitive, right?"

Jess said nothing. Brody was surprised at Naomi's approach, knowing most coaches of kids that age would have been all over the discipline of some sort. Was Naomi letting her off too easy?

"Because if you can't make that play, no other short-stops in this league are going to make it, either," she continued, extending an ego stroke Brody didn't think the girl necessarily deserved. Still, the kid picked up her hanging head.

"Yeah." The scrappy blonde had frustrated tears in her eyes. "But if Tyra can hit that, someone else on another team will be able to get one past me, too."

"So why don't you work in the practice field with Brody? I need to put Carrie in while you cool off anyway."

Sure enough, she'd yanked Jess from the scrimmage. But instead of being upset, the girl appeared grateful for the out and for the opportunity to work on her skills.

A true competitor.

"I'm right behind you," Brody told the kid as the pony-tailed blonde jogged by him and her teammates returned to the field. He lowered his voice as Naomi walked toward the third-base dugout near him. "Remind you of anyone?"

He knew his worst traits well enough to see himself in the kid.

"Yes. You're both the best players on your teams." She blew the whistle to start the next inning, clearing the bases to give the other team batting practice.

Brody shook his head.

"Come on. You know I'm talking about the temper problem." He didn't know where he'd picked up that explosiveness since none of his family members behaved that way, but it had gotten him in enough hot water in his life to know it wasn't attractive.

Hell, it could be his ticket to the unemployment line if his manager followed through on his promise to release him if he couldn't rein it in.

"Passionate on the field. Passionate off." She shrugged. "You're not the only person to get fired up about your game. If you ask me, you've got that fire to thank for where you are today."

"Are you kidding me?" He shook his head, half expecting her to make a crack about his temper. His teammates had started calling him Mercury the last time he'd gotten into it with an ump, as in his mercury rose faster than any other guy's in the line-up.

"Absolutely not." She pointed toward Jess. "She's going to practice fielding line drives until sunset, just the same way you practiced like a fiend when a ball got past you at home plate. I'll take Jess on my team any day."

She turned back toward the practice, shouting encouragement to a redhead at the plate who bit her lip in concentration every time the pitcher wound up.

As he walked away from Naomi and toward his preteen doppelganger, Brody wasn't really surprised at Naomi's easy going attitude, her acute understanding of human nature. Those qualities were only a portion of many reasons he should have never let her go in the first place.

With a woman like that at his side, maybe he wouldn't be spinning his wheels letting his temper railroad his career. Maybe he'd be letting the positive aspect of that—passion, she'd called it—fuel his ass forward in life. To be a better player.

Hell, maybe he could be a better person, too.

Picking up speed, he jogged toward where Jess waited, tossing herself fly balls and catching them on the run. Oh, yeah, Brody would help this girl with her game.

It was the least he could do since Jess had helped teach him a lesson he'd missed his whole adult life.

And considering that new understanding might be his ticket to feeling worthy of Naomi, the knowledge was pretty much priceless.

BRODY WAS MOBBED BY PARENTS after softball practice.

Naomi watched him try to make his way across the field to where she waited, sitting on the tailgate of her SUV. He signed autographs on auto club maps and fast food napkins—whatever the players' parents had handy when they picked up their kids. He'd also signed all the players' hats, leaving words of wisdom about the game on the insides of their brims.

Finally, he ambled over with his glove under his arm, his Aces ball cap jammed on his head backward.

"It's not quite like the crowd at the All-Star Game." She'd seen footage from the All-Star break enough times to know it was a media circus. Ticket prices were high, making the event less of a family affair and more geared toward the hardcore fans. "But they sure seemed pleased to have you here."

Especially Jess. Naomi had been really touched to see the way Brody coached her, demonstrating the fluid mechanics of the most economical throws to first, second, third and home. Far from being over her head, the information had been quickly put to good use by the young player, taking her skills up several notches in the course of a few hours. Naomi knew the girl would never forget the lessons she'd received from a world-class player.

"Your team is great." He tossed his glove in the truck and sat beside her on the tailgate. "I hope they beat the Braves Wednesday."

She laughed, amused at the vehemence in his voice.

"We'll do our best. Heaven knows if there are any line drives to the shortstop, we've got a guaranteed out."

"Jess is a quick study." He sat close to her so that his shoulder brushed hers. So that she couldn't forget the potent effect he had on her despite her wishes to the contrary. "You've done a great job with the team."

The simple praise touched her the way no extravagant compliment ever could have.

"Thank you." She cleared her throat, aware of the emotion clogging it. "You know how much I've always liked sports. Softball's my favorite, but I coach soccer, too."

"I've heard the kids in town all want to be on your teams." He peered out over the fields where another team had just started practice. There were four fields with a playground in the middle and a snack bar they ran during games that raised money for uniforms and new balls.

"You seem to hear a lot." She couldn't deny she was flattered about that.

"In particular, I heard you have some cool training films." He turned to her, one eyebrow lifted in question.

Heat crawled over her cheeks.

"I use game footage from the local colleges and the major leagues and put together a fun instructional video to get them pumped up." She kept her eyes trained on the monkey bars to avoid his gaze.

Unfortunately, he was having none of that. He cupped her cheek and turned her head toward him.

"I hear I've made the cut a few times."

Her heartbeat accelerated at the heat of his stare.

"Anybody who gets a play of the day in the nightly highlight reels is in the running for my video." She was a little defensive about it since Ryan had accused her of using her videos as an excuse to keep tabs on Brody's career. "Long before we dated, I was sneaking on my radio at night to listen to the late games when the Aces played on the West Coast. Mom still pitches in the women's league. My dad runs the men's. You must remember that we took a family vacation to Cuba once, just to see some games."

She took a breath, realizing she was rambling. Did she sound too defensive?

But Brody didn't look at her like she was trying to cover up some big, secret crush on him by taping a few of his best plays. Not like Ryan had. Brody watched her with something like admiration in his eyes.

"You love baseball. Just like me." He draped an arm around her shoulders, his thigh grazing hers. "You know how cool it is to talk to someone who understands the beauty of fielding a double play ball or the joy of fighting off impossible pitches to stay alive in the count when your team is down by a run in the last inning."

She smiled. "It's kind of like recognizing the skill of a five-tool player when you see Brody Davis knock one into the stands. Other fans see a two-run homer. I see the way you read the pitches and were ready for the curveball."

His lips brushed her temple in a tender kiss. For a moment, she absorbed the closeness of the moment, allowing her mind to entertain the prospect of being with him again. Of talking about baseball. Touring around the major league stadiums with him or spending days here at the rec field, coaching kids. They'd always had fun together. And their amazing chemistry translated into the most spectacular sex of her life.

All at once she realized what a fool she'd been to let him back into her life. She'd been kidding herself to think she'd be able to get him out of her system by spending the night with him. Instead of proving her memories of him were overrated, she'd only learned that being with him was better than she remembered.

"Brody." She eased away from him, needing to come back to reality before she got swept up in his world again, a world a long way from coastal New Hampshire.

But before she could explain why she needed to protect her heart, a truck pulled into the parking lot beside them, kicking up enough mud to spatter her shoes.

Incensed, she turned to tell the arriving parent to slow down. However, the silver Ford didn't belong to any player's family. She recognized the vehicle as the driver jammed the gearshift into Park and vaulted out of the cab.

Her ex-boyfriend, Ryan Patnode, strode around his truck to confront her. Actually, he appeared more like he planned to confront Brody since his eyes were glued to the Aces' catcher, his stare hostile.

Confrontational.

All at once, she realized how similar in temperament these two men were and she wondered for the first time if she'd gravitated toward Ryan for a very particular reason. Holy rebound man, they were even built similarly with tall, athletic bods.

Ryan jabbed a finger in Brody's chest and barked, "What the hell do you think you're doing?"

4

FOR A TEMPERAMENTAL GUY, Brody really hadn't been in many fights in his life.

He'd thrown a few punches back in Triple A when some redneck clown had threatened him with a broken beer bottle in retaliation for a flubbed play at the plate. And of course, there was the brawl seen around the world when he'd gotten into it with the Chicago Flames third basemen a few weeks ago. But other than that, he'd managed to keep his nose clean.

A feat he didn't see lasting much longer unless he did some fast talking.

The jerk pointing in his face was clearly looking for trouble.

"Lower your voice, Ryan," Naomi warned, peering past the newcomer toward the rec fields where a couple of young teams still ran their practices.

"So this is Ryan?" Brody clarified, understanding better why the guy was in a bad mood. "I didn't recognize you without your bicycle helmet."

He kept his arm around Naomi, figuring if his right hand was on her shoulder, he wouldn't be tempted to knock the jerk's accusatory finger into next year.

"Well, I recognize you, pretty boy, and if you don't get your hands off Naomi now I'm gonna show you how we settle disputes around here. And it doesn't involve a temper tantrum on home plate, I'll tell you that much."

Whoa. The guy wasn't just pissed to see another man touching his ex. This man was livid to see *Brody* touching his ex.

Apparently his style of baseball didn't appeal to the bicycle dude.

He was about to tell him to cool off when he realized Naomi had tensed beside him, her shoulders stiff as a board as she eased away from him.

"Ryan, we need to talk." She moved to slide off the tailgate.

Brody held her back. "Wait a minute." He looked at her, confused why she would take off with some angry jerk she'd already broken up with. "Do you see the vein ticking under this guy's eye? You can't go anywhere with someone this mad."

His request was reasonable. Hell, his request wasn't optional. He wasn't letting this woman—the woman he'd probably never stopped loving—spend time with a guy who went around threatening people.

For all that Brody had a temper on the field, he'd never dream of bringing it into his personal relationships.

"Don't you see what he's trying to do?" Naomi spoke quietly, eyes pleading for understanding as she met his gaze. "He wants to goad you into a fight for his fifteen minutes of fame. Or maybe so he can get you kicked out of baseball when the media hears about it."

Brody felt his eyebrows shoot up along with his skepticism.

"Give yourself more credit, Naomi." He didn't buy her theory for a minute. "Any guy who had you and lost you would be hurt to see you move on. I don't need to punch this guy. He already took a right hook to the chest just seeing me touch you."

But Naomi didn't seem to hear him. She turned her attention to her ex. Reaching for the finger the guy still poked at Brody's chest, she guided his hand down and away.

Just like that, the steam puffing the guy up seemed to hiss out of him. His shoulders sagged with defeat. His face fell. He sucked in a breath and Brody thought bicycle dude might cry.

If he was in Ryan's shoes, he might.

The poor bastard had lost more than a hot girlfriend when Naomi dumped him. He'd lost a caring, warm-hearted, amazing friend.

Still, recognizing that and empathizing with the loss didn't begin to feed the green monster that roared inside Brody when Naomi led Ryan a few feet away to talk privately. They weren't far from him in physical distance, but watching Naomi stand so close to another man, her face etched in lines of tender concern, made Brody feel a thousand miles away from her in every way that counted.

One of the teams' practices ended nearby and the parking lot started to fill with parents offering their kids advice or encouragement on how they'd played that day. Spikes sloshed through the muddy gravel lot, as the kids stowed their gear in trunks and shouted parting words to their friends. Brody sat apart from it all—unnoticed on the SUV tailgate with his hat pulled low. Not even the familiar sound of a bat pounding dirt out of mud-caked cleats could cheer him as he watched Naomi console her ex.

Did she want to get back together with the X-Gamer, even after that outburst? Hell, she'd stuck by Brody through enough shouting matches and had never seemed fazed.

But then, maybe Ryan felt like more of a real option for her since Brody hadn't come out and said he'd do whatever it took to make a future work for them. He'd been waiting for the right moment. And he'd almost arrived at it, but the bicycle dude had ruined it with crappy timing and bad attitude.

Unwilling to wait anymore for his shot at happiness, Brody slid off the tailgate and approached Naomi. He needed to speak to her now, before she patched things up with a guy who wasn't close to worthy of her.

His step slowed.

Was *he* worthy of her?

Brody would uproot her. Disrupt her teaching, her coaching, her whole life. And while he had a multi-million-dollar contract and a kick-ass lifestyle to offer, he knew she didn't care about stuff like that. His car didn't impress her any more than any of his other toys would.

Scrubbing a hand through his hair, he spun on his heel and stalked back to her vehicle. He couldn't afford to screw up her life when she had carved out a happy niche for herself here. He had no plan of attack and no inkling how he was any better for her than X-Game dude, who at least had the benefit of never having broken up with her via cell phone.

Dropping into the passenger seat of Naomi's SUV, he banged his head on the headrest and wondered where to go from here.

"THANK YOU FOR LETTING ME talk to him."

Naomi finally broke the silence on their way back to her place after the embarrassing encounter with Ryan at the practice field.

She'd taken the long way home, both to clear her head and because she remembered Brody liked the view of the Atlantic from a bluff they would pass in another few minutes.

She felt a need to make it up to him after the way she'd ditched him at the field to talk Ryan off the emotional ledge. Things had ended on an ugly note with him a few weeks ago and she'd managed to avoid him until today. No doubt seeing her with Brody had hurt.

"You have a knack for calming down ticked off guys," he observed lightly, his gaze trained out the window at the sun warming the wet fields after the downpour the night before.

"I figured he deserved to know how I felt about you since he had accused me of being hung up on you." Her heart pounded with the admission and the scariness of laying it on the line with Brody.

But why avoid the truth?

Brody straightened in his seat, his gaze rounding on her as she approached the turnoff for a scenic lookout point over the ocean.

"So you told *him* how you feel, but not me?" He sounded incensed.

Slowing to a stop, she put the SUV in Park.

"Consider it payback." She swiveled in her seat to face him, prepared to have it out with him once and for all. "According to you, you really cared about me a year ago and didn't bother telling me. Instead you let me think I meant nothing to you."

This man had broken her heart, and while he might have had mildly good intentions for what he'd done, his approach had sucked. If she was going to make peace with their past, she would at least call him on the behavior and—just maybe—give him a glimpse into how it had made her feel.

Apparently the glimpse had rendered him speechless

because he stared at her in disbelief, his gorgeous mouth falling open so that she reached to lift his jaw for him.

"Don't you remember?" she prodded, turning to roll down her window a little more so the fresh seaside air could blow through. "You told me last night that letting you stay could be my revenge. I could be the one to walk away."

"And you're taking me up on it." His jaw flexed. His eyebrows scrunched up. His words were clipped.

They were all the signs she remembered from when she'd seen him get mad. Which was just as well, because she was dead serious about the payback.

"You gave me no freaking clue about your motives for breaking up with me last year. None. And then you show up at my door twelve months later and say it was all for my own good?" She'd had time to think about it during softball practice this morning and she still couldn't swallow his tactics. If he thought he could just waltz in and out of her life this way, he was sadly mistaken.

Even if he did make her feel things no other man had ever come close to inspiring.

A flash of hurt in his eyes nearly undid her. But just as quickly, he shuttered his expression and thrust out his stubborn jaw.

"It was for your own good. And mine. And so is this." He reached over to her side of the vehicle and withdrew her keys from the ignition.

"What are you doing?" She made a grab for them.

He arced back and with the strength and speed that could gun down a runner trying to steal second, he pitched her keys out the window. They went sailing into the woods where she'd be lucky to ever find them.

"I'm showing you that I'm not going anywhere." The mutinous expression on his face was the same one he'd flashed umpires from Little League right up through the ranks.

"Oh, no, you don't." Wrenching open the door to her SUV, she stepped out to go search for her keys. "You can get away with that crazy, temperamental guy stuff on the baseball field because you've got skills every manager wants. But this is *me*." She started marching away from the SUV, her voice raised so he didn't miss a word. "You're not so all-mighty damn important that you can toss me aside when you think it's best or pitch some unholy fit to make me do what you want."

She stomped toward the tree line, carried along by righteous indignation.

He was out of the vehicle and jogging beside her in two seconds flat.

"This is not a fit." He planted his body in front of hers, blocking her path. "This is making you see reason."

It wasn't the obstacle of his formidable frame that stopped her. It was the look in his eyes. He wasn't mad. He was all business.

All passionate drive and intensity.

This time, it was her who was speechless. He stepped forward, backing her up toward her SUV.

"I didn't come here to mess this up again." He kept walking toward her until she bumped into the side of her vehicle. With nowhere else to go, she faced him down while he bracketed her with his arms. "I came here to snap you up while you weren't dating anyone else. I came to tell you that I've never cared about anyone as much as you."

Her heart sort of turned over inside her, its furious beat slowing as Brody looked into her eyes. His body was so close she could feel the heat of him and smell the musky notes of aftershave that had tantalized her the night before.

"How can I trust that?" she asked, feeling weak inside. "You've been back in my life for twenty-four hours."

It would be so easy to go along with him, to ride the tide of his hunger for her and let it sweep her to the sweet, amazing heights. But where would it leave her in the end?

"You can trust it because you aren't the kind of person to condemn a guy forever for the stupid stuff he did at a time in his life when he didn't have his head screwed on straight."

She wasn't, either.

"How can you know me so freaking well when we haven't seen each other in so long?"

He skimmed a knuckle under her chin, as light as the breeze blowing off the water.

"Because I dated you longer than anyone else. Because we went to the prom together. We formed a template for each other about what we wanted in a partner just by being each other's first romantic interests." He grinned. "Don't you watch Oprah?"

She nearly choked on a laugh. His goofy admission made her love him even though he'd just pitched her keys two miles into the brush. He was so impossible to resist.

"Okay. Let's say I buy into that and, for argument's sake, let's say I'm crazy enough to fall for you all over again in spite of everything." Just saying the words made her heart beat faster, the emotions for him surging inside her like a rogue wave. "How do you expect to make a relationship work when you play 162 games a year and are traveling the country from March until October?"

A professional baseball player's life—while exciting—hardly lent itself to a committed relationship with someone who had roots and ties to a community.

His cell phone rang then, an obnoxious intrusion into an important conversation. She suspected if they ever tried to make it work between them, there would be a lot of that.

Brody didn't move to answer it.

"Aren't you going to get that?"

"This is more important." He ignored the second ring, too.

"What if it's your team?"

If anything, it had been a miracle that the device hadn't been ringing off the hook all night, but maybe he'd powered it down to get away from the media requests for interviews and general industry excitement.

"You're more important to me than baseball." He paused long and deliberately after that statement, and she recognized it for exactly what it meant.

He couldn't have told her he loved her with any more emphasis than what he'd just said.

Her heart did backflips. Her knees sort of fell out from under her and she launched herself into his arms. Whatever else happened, whatever they could or couldn't work out, Brody loved her.

Enough to ignore a multi-million-dollar career.

"I love you, too." She sort of sobbed it into his shirt, a surprise shower of happy tears raining down her cheeks that this passionate, incredible man would put her before everything else in his life. Still, on the fourth ring, she dug in his pocket and took out his phone. "But you aren't giving up baseball for me, Brody Davis."

Flipping open the cell, she pressed it to his ear.

"Hello? Jeff? Um…can you hold on a sec?" He took the phone away from her and held it behind his back, ignoring his caller. "Naomi, I don't want to screw this up. Staying in baseball would mean a lot of travel."

She couldn't believe he would discuss this *now*.

"Is that your manager on the line?" She felt a little starstruck to think baseball legend Jeff Rally might be waiting on hold.

"Yes. But don't think about that. Think about how you'd feel to travel with a major league team, never coming back here except for Christmas." He frowned, the worry evident in his furrowed brow. "I can't ask you to give up your career any more than you would ask me to give up mine."

Naomi clutched his shoulders, her heart soaring to think about the kind of future they might have together.

"With you in the lineup, we have a shot at the pennant." She spoke slowly so he'd remember how important that was. "I have the best interests of you, me and every Boston fan in the world in mind when I tell you that I can take a hiatus from teaching to cheer you on for as long as you can swing a bat."

The lines on his forehead smoothed away and he wrapped an arm around her to pull her close.

"I am so crazy about you, sweetheart." He planted a kiss on her lips that reminded her how much she'd be gaining by going on the road with him. "I swear you won't ever regret this."

"I know I won't," she assured him, grabbing his arm and wrenching it up so he could finish his phone call. "Now don't keep a baseball legend waiting any longer."

In her heart, she knew that Brody's manager wouldn't release him for the previous day's offense. He'd been out of line, but not *that* out of line. Jeff Rally was known for running a tight ship, so it made sense that he'd at least throw the threat out there. But Rally hadn't been in the game for most of his life by being the kind of manager who released players with a .660 slugging percentage.

And sure enough, her guess was confirmed by Brody's easy smile, his heartfelt apology, and his promise to be on the plane to Baltimore by nightfall.

But then, that was something she understood about Brody. He could get upset and yell, but just as quickly as the storm cloud of temper came, it would be gone again. And he was as sincere in his apologies as he was with his outbursts. It was part of his charm, and she hoped the media and his fans would come to recognize the way this passionate, driven man could do more than just hit and field the ball. His bouts of anger could fire up team members who weren't playing with heart. Brody Davis could fuel a whole field to excel.

When he closed the phone, he dropped it back in his pocket.

"Looks like we're headed to Baltimore." He wrapped his arms around her. "I can't believe you'd go with me."

The rightness of her decision filled her.

"It's August. There's enough time to find a teacher to take my classes before school starts. And I think the kids I coach will forgive me for bailing on them a week before their season ends if I come up with some Aces tickets for a field trip." She allowed herself to sink into his arms. Into the moment. "Too bad you tossed my keys into the middle of the woods where we'll never find them again. You'll have to walk to Baltimore at this rate."

"Geez, woman." He kissed the top of her head and stroked a possessive hand along her spine. "I understand you inside and out and you don't know me at all."

"What do you mean?" She tipped away from him to gauge his expression.

"I make that play an average of five times a night, five

times a week." He took her by the hand and pulled her toward the woods, counting off his paces as they walked.

"You think you'll find those keys?" She rather hoped so because she couldn't wait to start their new life. Together.

"Second base is 127 feet and change from home. And I've got killer aim. So as long as we stay in a straight line…" He ducked beneath a low-hanging branch as they entered the tree line. And right on cue, she could see the glint of silver ahead, among the pine needles and fallen leaves. "We'll find them right where second base would be."

Laughing, she picked them up, jingling their weight on her finger. "Except you didn't account for the lack of rotation like a baseball would have, or the non-aerodynamic shape. I think you're pushing it to suggest you got more than 110 feet."

"And I think you forgot just what a rocket I've got for a right arm." He looped his arms around her again and she was half tempted to pinch herself to make sure that today had been real. "But I don't mind working harder to prove myself to you."

She stretched on her toes to brush a kiss along his bristly jaw.

"You already made my personal highlight film. I know you're pretty damn amazing."

He pulled her hips to his, the heat of him already warming her body in the most delicious way.

"I've got another highlight film I want to make though." Leaning down, he nipped her ear and backed her against the trunk of an old locust tree.

"Oh, really?"

"Actually a few of them. I think we'll start with top ten lovemaking moments." He picked her up and wrapped her legs around his waist. "Then we can work on top ten shower scenes. Most memorable ways to put my mouth to work—"

"Oh, my." She thought she might overheat despite the ocean breeze.

"You know how I like to set the record in whatever I do."

Her heart fluttered fast as she thought about the life he wanted for them. Being part of Brody's world was going to be purely magical. Not because he was a big deal baseball player, but because he was a warm-hearted person who had never stopped caring about her. A passionate man who was ready to devote himself to her.

Tunneling her fingers through his hair, she pulled him close.

"Have I told you how much I love a man with a competitive streak?" She melted into a slow tangle of tongues she would put at the very top of her list for the best kisses she'd ever had the pure pleasure to receive.

SQUEEZE PLAY

1

SCRAPERS' MONTERO NO STRANGER to New York's Most Wanted List.

Lance Montero re-read the headline on a summary sheet from his publicist as he downed his morning espresso at the trendy new coffee shop across the street from his Manhattan apartment building.

His romantic eligibility status had landed him in some social column about the city's bachelors. Which wasn't a big deal on its own, but the piece had been picked up all over the country and generated a slew of personal articles about him.

That, in turn, made it look like his focus wasn't on his game. The Scrapers' manager had called him in for a meeting about it after the All-Star break, grilling him about his level of commitment to the team. To making the playoffs.

And damn, did that tick him off. If you ignored the press, you were labeled as inaccessible and not a "team player." But if you attracted too much notice, you were a media hog.

"Can I get you anything else?"

The waitress returned to his end of the coffeehouse, her dark pantsuit a staple of the employees.

But she wasn't the same waitress he'd had earlier. Her throaty voice wasn't the same chipper soprano that had greeted him at five this morning and her perfume was subtle but distinct to a man who noticed that kind of thing. In fact, it was the appeal of her scent that pulled his nose out of the PR report he'd been reviewing.

Petite and brunette, the woman now holding the espresso carafe was drop-dead gorgeous if you were into the sexpot type. Which Lance wasn't. Especially not when he planned to quit dating until after the postseason.

"No, thank you. That'll do it." He withdrew his wallet and dropped a few bills on the table, realizing the brew house had grown far more crowded since he'd entered. Maintaining a low profile wasn't easy for a player in the city that never slept, but Lance worked hard to avoid heavy traffic times at establishments like this in order to stay out of the papers.

In order to live down his undeserved reputation as some kind of lothario and direct attention back to his career.

"You sure are cute," the waitress observed, setting the espresso carafe on the table before looking over her shoulder. As if confident no one was close enough to overhear her, she leaned down to speak more softly. "How come there are never any good-looking, normal guys like you sitting alone in a coffee shop whenever *I* go out?"

Lance grinned because, even though he was swearing off dating, what guy didn't enjoy open flirtation with an attractive woman? Especially one who viewed him as a "normal guy" and not a target on some enterprising woman's list of most eligible bachelors. Her shoulder-length dark hair slid down to fall alongside them, curtaining them in privacy for a moment. He noticed her gold name tag read Jamie.

"I don't know." He folded his wallet and shoved it in his jacket pocket. "How come I never run into any nice girls who smell as good as you do when I'm in the market for a date?"

She nodded as if she understood completely. Her eyes betrayed no hint of recognition that he was a baseball player or anyone who looked vaguely familiar, and he couldn't help but enjoy the anonymity of the encounter. Too often, women hit on him because of who he was.

The only reason he'd gotten a reputation as a playboy was because he sucked at recognizing the women who were only after his checkbook until he'd been out with them a few times. And why should he keep dating that kind of person just to clear his name in the press as someone who couldn't maintain a relationship?

"I guess we're victims of bad timing." Her smile glittered with old-school lip gloss that looked good enough to eat, and underneath the sheen was a pair of lips that could have been an advertisement for collagen injections.

Women would pay big bucks for the pouty, bee-stung mouth she sported naturally. Not that he was mentally making plans for those lips or anything. Just a casual observation.

"My friends say it's that I hit on all the wrong women." Standing, he pulled on a cap with the name of an NFL team to throw off people who might recognize him.

The sexy server, Jamie, clutched her chest, her black V-neck blouse framing a soft swell of cleavage and a gold necklace with the initials JM.

"Are your friends in league with mine? My traitorous crew says I'm a magnet for man trouble."

"Good thing I didn't just hit on you, Jamie M, or I'd be mighty offended." He meant to walk out on that note, but something about the brimming good humor in her big brown eyes kept him rooted to the spot.

She looked at him like they shared a secret and he

looked at her like—he couldn't stop. Damn, but he'd missed that feeling. That genuine spark that flared between two people for no discernable reason, the invisible electricity that crackled when your brain read a hundred pleasing signals in someone else and—though you haven't had time to process them yet—your mind won't let you walk away without more careful consideration.

Her hand went to her necklace as if she'd forgotten it was there, her eyes never leaving his while they stood together in the back room of the restaurant where a few tables surrounded a fireplace.

From the corner of his eye, Lance spied movement in the short hall that connected the room to the rest of the establishment and he figured he'd better hit the closest exit. It was past 7:00 a.m. and the commuter crowd was out in full force judging by the noise.

He nodded a goodbye that was probably unnecessary, but the movement in the hallway grew loud and bright before he took two steps back. A flood lamp on wheels drenched the room in light. A small camera crew followed shortly behind it.

For a moment, Lance wondered why the media would be hounding him around his home since he hadn't done anything unusual lately to spark extra interest. Sure, maybe some chick magazine would stake out his place to see where he went at night and if the city's eligible bachelor had a date, but why a TV camera at seven in the morning?

But then, he became aware of the hot waitress yelling at the cameraman, waving the espresso pot in a threatening gesture.

"Do you have to follow me everywhere?" She gripped the pole for the flood lamp and swiveled it away from them, effectively wrecking the footage. "I'm doing this for *charity,* pinheads, not to finance your next trip to Fiji. So you can take your little money-hungry selves and—"

"Hey, Jamie," a guy shouted from behind the camera while Lance tried to blink the spots from his vision. "Are you seeing Lance Montero now?"

Uh-oh.

He'd been recognized. And if he was reading the signs correctly, apparently his waitress was no stranger to the media. In fact, judging by the relationship she seemed to have with the camera crew, he suspected she wasn't just your average waitress, either.

"Who?" She turned on him, some of her spunky anger for the paparazzi coming at him now, her lips pursed in a tight frown.

Before Lance could answer, a coffee shop patron wearing a Scrapers hat stood up and waved a cell phone at the guy behind the camera.

"I've got the whole thing on my video phone. These two just met a minute ago."

Lance's jaw dropped at the string of bad luck. He'd wanted to quit dating to keep his romantic life on the down low, and in short order, he'd flirted with a woman who was some sort of media target, and he'd been caught on tape by a TV crew and some bozo who would probably post the video on YouTube before Lance got home.

The throng started firing questions at the waitress, and she arced her arm back like she was seriously considering firing the espresso carafe at one of the reporters' heads.

Crap.

Knowing he was going to look like a damn deer in headlights on the highlight reel, Lance plotted damage control. Grabbing Jamie M by the hand, he pulled her toward the fire exit in the back and left the crowd behind.

"WHO THE HELL ARE YOU?"

Jamie had trotted out better lines than that one in the past when she'd met a cute guy, but she wasn't terribly concerned about what this man thought of her since he'd just hijacked her from her latest goodwill publicity stunt intended to clean up her trashed reputation. Who was he?

Someone had blurted out the name *Lance Montero* at the diner, but it didn't mean much to her.

"I might ask *you* the same question."

The hottie who had been flirting with her moments ago now steered her down the street with his big, gorgeous body, never asking her where she'd like to go. He'd slung a possessive arm around her at some point, and navigated through the gross back alley that smelled like refuse to pause at the side door of some major high rise. He reached for the knob as if to escort her inside.

"I don't think so." She dug in the heels of her three-inch wedge espadrilles—metaphorically speaking, since the pavement didn't come close to giving way under her feet.

"You don't think I'm entitled to know who you are?" He hauled open the door with one hand and tugged a security card out of his wallet with the other one, as if he anticipated more doors to open.

"I think you're not entitled to corral me into some unknown building just because I let you escort me out of the diner."

The man was incredibly good-looking with his close-cropped dark hair and melted chocolate-brown eyes. He was tall and buff, a fact she knew from being sheltered under his arm when he'd rushed her out of the coffeehouse. He dressed like some kind of Wall Street executive with an expensive silk suit and a shirt she'd bet was custom made, but his tie was aquamarine and yellow—an artsy statement for a financial dude. Maybe Lance Montero was the new Donald Trump.

Not that she was in the market for a guy with big bucks. In her experience, men with money often came with an inflated sense that the world was theirs for the taking.

"I thought I was helping you out back there." He relinquished the door and peered over his shoulder, as if he expected the camera crew to come chasing them down the narrow side street.

"Hardly. I'm trying to raise money for charity." Who was this guy that he could be so oblivious? Maybe he'd had his nose buried in a newspaper when he walked in the coffee shop that morning. "Didn't you see the signs all over the java place advertising the celebrity fundraiser?"

Ever since her divorce, she'd become one of the most recognizable women in the country thanks to her ex's efforts to paint her as a spoiled socialite. And admittedly, a small bout of bad behavior on her part. But she'd been in an unhappy place during her divorce. She still found it difficult to scrounge up much regret for the catfight she'd landed in with her ex's skanky chick on the side.

Of course, she'd regret it even less if it hadn't been caught on video by someone in the crowd. And if that person hadn't posted it online. And most especially, if her halter top had remained in place throughout the minibrawl. Her bare boobs had an embarrassingly high hit count.

Yet it seemed like the *GQ*-worthy stud in front of her had no clue who she was despite her notoriety. Then again, she'd only been famous because of her mega-bucks family prior to her marriage, despite her best attempts to distance herself from being billed as an oil heiress. Who wanted to be known for the environment-destroying wealth buried under your granddaddy's corn field? It was ludicrous. Her attempts at launching a career as a folk singer often got lost in favor of her family name.

And because of her occasional lapses in good behavior.

Now she'd fallen into a brand-new drama with someone else whose celebrity would drag her into the spotlight for the wrong reasons.

He frowned.

"I went in through the back—the same way we left. I usually try to avoid the morning rush." He smoothed his tie and adjusted the newspaper under his arm, the same one he'd been reading in the restaurant. The journal had been folded to the sports section, with a photo from a baseball game peeking out from behind his elbow.

"Well, I made a commitment to work at the event today and I can't back out just because some of the more irritating members of the media hoped I would stir up trouble." Did they really think she'd get into a knockdown, drag-out fight at a fundraising event?

She retreated a step, ignoring the vibrating cell phone in her back pocket. No doubt someone had ratted her out to her agent who would be ticked off about her hasty exit from the charity gig.

"The media thought you would stir up trouble," he parroted back at her, his expression morphing to thinly veiled disapproval instead of the normal curiosity or interest that usually came when people found out they were speaking to a celebrity. "Jamie M. That must stand for—"

"McRae." She thrust out a hand and shook his before he offered it. "Jamie McRae. Nice to meet you, Mr. Enigmatic."

His expression shifted again, this time moving from the earlier disapproval to something she'd categorize as vague horror.

"You're that big music producer's wife. The one who got in the catfight and lost her top."

"I didn't *lose* it. It was forcefully *yanked* from my body by a woman who hates my guts. And I'm the music producer's *ex*-wife, by the way." She thought the whole world knew about her well-publicized split. But maybe some people had missed the details in favor of the more exciting headline that she'd exposed a nipple in a ritzy Hollywood bar.

Before Lance could explain why he was staring at her as if she was his worst nightmare, she heard the oncoming rush of feet and voices, a sure sign their alone time was over.

Whipping the newspaper out from under his arm, he handed it to her.

"Then we're screwed."

The page featured a face shot of the man in front of her along with a picture of him sliding into home plate, his fist raised in the air victoriously. It was no game in a men's Over-Thirty League. This was big time. The majors. The guy was wearing a New York Scrapers uniform with the trademark Empire State Building silhouette and Manhattan skyline.

She had been caught on film flirting with one of New York's favorite sons, the legendary playmaker Lance Montero.

A name anyone else in the city would have known immediately, but as a recent L.A. transplant, Jamie had been slow on the uptake. There had been a time when she wouldn't have minded a little harmless flirtation to encourage her husband to pay attention to her. But that was before she learned he'd lavished all his attention on other women instead of work, as he'd claimed.

He yanked the paper back. "You're about to have your past splashed all over the headlines and I'm—" He scowled. "I'll be written off yet again as the playboy ladies' man who spends more time playing the field than—er—playing the field."

He didn't need to explain it. The consequences were crystal clear to her. She was about to have a media nightmare reprised and she had no doubt that he'd be raked over the coals for dating someone like her—someone with a reputation for speaking her mind in the press.

"Take cover," she warned him, shoving his big, sexy body toward his building. "I'll deal with the fallout since I've got to resurface over there anyhow."

Tucking the newspaper into her purse, she searched her brain for how to spin the encounter for the media as the first camera appeared around a corner. She'd developed a bit of a knack for this crap over the last six months.

"If you're sure—" His chocolate-brown eyes shuttered at the arrival of the invading lenses and she knew a moment's regret that they'd met under such crappy circumstances.

Then she remembered that he was definitely the wrong type of guy for her. Wealthy beyond imagining. A media favorite. And if memory served—a confirmed heartbreaker.

"Positive." With one last push to his shoulder, she finally succeeded in budging him. Or maybe he simply acquiesced.

Either way, she was alone by the time the press arrived in full force to barrage her with questions. And withdrawing her favorite leopard-print umbrella from her purse, she popped it open and took cover behind the nylon. Then, cruising through the streets like a ship at full sail, she navigated her way through the worst of it the way she'd plowed through so much other garbage ever since she'd become a notorious woman.

Although her methods were slick and savvy, her public veneer as tough as ever, Jamie couldn't help but mourn the loss of a private life. Especially on a day when she'd crossed paths with the most intriguing man she'd met in a long, long time.

2

WHAT A WOMAN.

Lance couldn't get Jamie out of his mind that night as he reached for a fresh bat before his turn in the on-deck circle. He hadn't been able to resist a glance out the tinted windows of his building at her after he'd left her to fend for herself with the media hounds. He'd half regretted leaving her there all alone even though she'd seemed desperate for him to get lost. But any worries he'd had about her had vanished when he'd seen that umbrella snap open, cocooning her in leopard-print privacy.

No doubt about it, she was a pro at dealing with the press.

As the crowd at Scrapers Stadium cheered for a hit by the lead-off batter, Lance grinned all over again at the memory of the way Jamie had run full tilt through the paparazzi before they could pen her in with microphones and questions. Her moves were sweeter than an NFL running back as she'd dodged hits from every side, finding the holes in the defense to make it up field. He'd been cheering her progress all the way back to the coffee shop.

Of course, he'd been less pleased when he returned to his penthouse apartment to already find an e-mail from his publicist with a link to the online video of his morning flirtation with Jamie. He'd watched the video and instead of being embarrassed by the encounter he'd been taken in by her sexy grin all over again. But that link had been accompanied by a slew of other video snippets. Some were amusing enough, like the time the Texas oil heiress hitchhiked across the Lone Star State with a camcorder and a mission to uncover more "green" energy options, much to the irritation of her father.

But the video with the most links and the most hype appeared to be the wrestling match with her ex-husband's girlfriend—a recording he didn't watch out of respect for her. Beyond that, there seemed to be a whole list of film bites alluding to impulsive behavior, but he could read between the lines enough to see they were amateur bits probably filmed by people trying to aggravate her into losing her cool. At the bottom of all that, he found a few videos for music she'd written to benefit a variety of environmental causes. He'd had to dig to find those, however, since her personal life seemed to overshadow the rest. She actually had a great voice.

Fingers snapping in front of his nose wrenched his thoughts away from Jamie.

"You got your head in the game, Montero?" a voice from the bench piped up as Lance climbed the steps to leave the dugout. "We need this one."

They were playing the Boston Aces tonight, a rivalry that stretched back to when the league was in its infancy and tickets to a day game cost pocket change. Boston had beaten them out in the playoffs the previous year, but New York had spent big bucks on some rookie talent to improve their chances this year. One of whom just had a base hit with two outs in the bottom of the seventh. The Scrapers were down by two, so the runner on first could be the tying score.

"Is my head in the game?" Lance turned toward the lineup on the bench, staring down his teammates. He normally minded his own business with the other players, but in a youth-dominated sport, sometimes it paid to defend your territory and put the mouthy ones in their place. Narrowing in on the perpetrator, he leveled his bat in the guy's direction. "Bobcat, you work on that hole in your glove and let the big guns take care of the hits."

He grinned as he stalked off to the on-deck circle for a few warm up swings, keeping things on friendly footing. Of course, half the team hooted at the taunt while the other half smothered laughs. The right fielder had bobbled one early in the second inning that cost the Scrapers a run, and no doubt big Bob Cacciatore would be stinging from that error all week. But if he couldn't handle the ribbing, he damn well shouldn't dish it out.

In the meantime, the hitter walked, advancing the leadoff runner and bringing Lance up to bat. The crowd reaction was predictable—he'd been sent to the All-Star Game for five years straight. But he had die-hard detractors along with his fans. This was New York, after all. No major league city was more notorious for tough fans.

And tonight they seemed louder than ever. Or maybe that was because Boston's supporters didn't mind traveling to cheer on their team. Scrapers Stadium sported plenty of Boston blue and red this evening. And as Lance readjusted the Velcro straps on his batting gloves, he noticed a crowd of Boston fans featured on the overhead screen. That in itself wasn't unusual.

What was out of the ordinary is that the whole row of guys wearing Aces T-shirts also held up paper copies of Jamie McRae's gorgeous face in front of their own. The jumbotron broadcast ten identical smiling Jamies for the whole stadium to see.

One of the hecklers waved a sign that read "Boston's

Secret Weapon is the Catfight Queen." The guy next to him flashed a piece of cardboard that said "Jamie McRae—the Ultimate Distraction" next to a cartoon of Lance with eyes the size of dinner plates and a head that looked like a bobble head doll.

Is your head in the game, Lance?

Bobcat's question suddenly didn't seem so off base as the noise in the stadium rose to a fever pitch.

Damn. It.

A hundred-mile-an-hour fastball suddenly seemed like the best place for him to take out his frustration. He'd been trying to polish up his womanizer image and he'd inadvertently flirted with a notorious divorcée in front of the whole world. But that was the nature of the media, wasn't it? One mistake could alter the course of a career.

And the only defense Lance had against the hooting and hollering crowd was to send that fastball into the East River. A simple matter of physics and iron will.

Too bad the first ball got past him.

And the second.

Down in the count, he half regretted talking smack to Bobcat. How could he brag about getting hits when he watched two fastballs sail past him without getting the bat on a square millimeter of it?

Careers were made or broken at moments like this. And it wouldn't have jack squat to do with a strikeout and everything to do with a sexy songbird who had taken up residence in his head—and in the public eye— at the worst possible time.

Seeing the potential career-defining moment in front of him, Lance realized Jamie McRae wasn't going away simply because he ignored her. Like it or not, the two of them were forever linked by an unguarded moment caught on film.

Digging in at home plate, Lance tightened his grip on the bat and stared down the hard-ass pitcher with a left arm like a cannon. Lance kept his eye on the ball as it left the guy's hand and swung for the fences.

When the splitter hit the bat, it wasn't a crack that would send it to the East River, but Lance knew beyond a doubt it was a hit that would end up in the stands. The solid connection of his time-tested Louisville Slugger on the ball was the kind of beautiful moment a player never forgot. Even on his home field where he'd hit one out plenty of times.

There was magic playing under the lights for seventy-five thousand fans at one of the biggest baseball stadiums in the world. And something about having all those people there to witness it, driving the ball deep into the opposite field against one of the best pitchers in the majors, tattooed this particular three-run homer forever in his mind.

Jogging the bases, Lance noticed the jumbotron had stopped showing the hecklers with Jamie photos, swapping instead to fireworks and all kinds of home run graphics. But he didn't need to see Jamie with his eyes to see her in his head because—even with a clutch at bat behind him—Lance knew his head had never been in the game tonight. He wouldn't rest until he'd tracked down Jamie and explored the connection between them— because it wasn't going away just by ignoring it.

HER PHONE WOULDN'T STOP ringing just because she ignored it.

Jamie knew this from experience since she'd ignored every call she'd received after the latest media maelstrom had blown through her life, aka Lance Montero. But she definitely couldn't take any calls right now when the source of her latest problems might put in an appearance any moment.

She'd been waiting for him in the players' parking lot for the last twenty minutes. It was easy enough to get into the area where the home team parked their cars, although there were loads of security guards around to make sure people passing through didn't touch the sleek, high-end automobiles the athletes favored. A few members of the media milled around the door where the players would exit into the garage, but Jamie had avoided their notice by wearing a false nose she'd purchased for an old Halloween costume. It wasn't the first time she'd used the fake schnoz. Between the prosthetic, a hat and some sunglasses, she was fairly safe as long as she didn't mingle.

"Here he comes," someone shouted near the doors.

An answering rustle of excitement surged through the throng as floodlights clicked on and last-minute audio feeds were tested. Jamie hung back, sticking close to Lance's car in the hope she could ride out of here with him. As much as she wanted to put the kibosh on the media interest in their nonrelationship, she knew that couldn't be done without some help from him. And she had a plan to make it happen that would serve them both well.

Still, an unexpected flutter of excitement went through her at the thought of seeing him again and she marveled at the surprising chemistry they'd experienced. Not that she could listen to her instincts when it came to men. Especially powerful men with a foot in the spotlight. She'd been dragged through that wringer before and didn't plan to go back for seconds, no matter how enticing the baseball player looked in a suit.

The hubbub around the door increased and then she spotted him. Tall and commanding, he dwarfed most of the media members. He had to be all of six foot three, his shoulders easily wedging their way through pedestrian traffic toward the low-slung Viper that one of the security guards had confided belonged to him. The information hadn't been difficult to come by as the security officer had been all of twenty years old and easily impressed by a suggestive glimpse of thigh.

Jamie could have upped the size of her nose times three and she'd still bet a tight skirt would have yielded information. It was one of those endearing quirks of the male species that they were hardwired to respond to a woman's legs.

"I can't right now," the shortstop star was saying to one of the reporters, keeping his responses brief and his feet moving.

"Do you have a date with Jamie McRae?" one of the camera wielders shouted over the din of other questions. "Did you know about her infamous past before you met?"

"How long have you known each other?" someone else asked.

"Did you hit that three-run homer for her tonight?" another pressed.

"The hit was for the team," he replied, calm and charming in the face of ten microphones aimed for his mouth.

His movement toward the car brought the throng with him like a swarm of bees, the noise level rising with their proximity. Jamie hoped she could find a way to slide into the car without much fuss, but the closer he came, the more difficult it seemed. She'd been proud of herself for slipping her own press. She hadn't fully prepared for confronting his.

And it was formidable.

Panicked, she sidled closer to the passenger-side door as Lance noticed her. She could tell the instant he spotted her since she felt his eyes on her clear down to her toes like a physical caress. A man's glance should never have that much power over a woman. But the butterflies in Jamie's stomach picked up their jittery dance at one look from those melted chocolate eyes of his.

And damned if he didn't see right past the fake nose, the sunglasses and the hat. The shift in his expression from coolly determined to surprised and curious was as plain as the oversize nose on her face.

At least, she hoped she was reading him correctly.

There might be hell to pay if she jumped into his car uninvited. Not that she hadn't danced with the devil a time or two in her day.

"Get in," he ordered, pressing a button on his key remote that sounded a *click* of the doors unlocking. The engine rumbled to life before he reached the vehicle, a trick of a remote starter.

Hurrying to do as he asked while all eyes in the parking garage turned to her, Jamie slid into the passenger seat and locked herself side. Slumping down in the seat to avoid the sea of camera lenses swinging in her direction, she admired Lance's easy athleticism and economy of movement as he folded himself into the driver seat. He put the car in Reverse before the door was even shut.

"We meet again," he observed lightly, flipping down her sun visor to help shield her face from the spectators beginning to recognize her.

"I had no idea you'd be so mobbed after a game or I would have found another way to get in touch with you."

The garage's security staff was already moving the crowd to one side, clearly accustomed to protecting the players from this kind of thing.

"You failed to notice what an uproar our first meeting

created?" He whipped the car around as soon as he had enough room to maneuver.

Wasting no time, he jammed down on the gas pedal and steered them around to the upper levels where an attendant waved them through to an exit that would put them on the West Side Highway. They were as good as home free.

Jamie pulled off her nose and swiped away the thin film of stage makeup that had held it in place. Depositing it into her bag, she hit the ignore button on her cell phone for the umpteenth time that day.

"Actually, I've worked hard not to notice since I've had all the bad news I can handle this year." Tipping her head back onto the seat rest, she allowed herself a moment to enjoy the speed of the luxury sports car, the motor humming with the smooth accent of superb foreign engineering. The scent of leather and a subtle bay rum aftershave soothed her.

The thought triggered a frisson of warning down her neck. How could she feel so calm in the presence of a powerful, moneyed man? Would she ever learn her lesson where these kinds of guys were concerned? Straightening, she shook off the sweet languor and resurrected a few protective barriers.

Well, she did place her oversize purse on the console between them.

"So you avoided the news all day, but you didn't avoid me." He turned to flash a quick wink before focusing once again on the road. "I like that."

Her heart skipped a beat at his easy flirtation. He had a charm that drew her in without making her feel pressured or like he was giving her the hard sell. There was something warm and genuine about the man despite his fame and his millions.

"About that—"

"I wanted to see you again, too."

Now her heart skipped more than a beat. It seemed to miss a whole sequence, freezing her in place for a moment while she tried to absorb what those words meant. How could such a simple statement carry so much impact?

And how could the city's favorite son want to hang out with the country's breast-baring scarlet woman?

"You did?" The vital organ that halted a moment ago now beat with renewed flurry, making her all jittery inside.

She shoved all thought of her plan for containing this mess aside to hear him out.

"Definitely." He sounded resolved, his jaw locked in a determined jut as she stared at his profile. "I'll admit it probably doesn't make sense for either of us on paper. And I'm sorry your split from your ex put you through such a public ordeal. But I couldn't get you out of my head today and I don't think ignoring what happened between us is going to make it disappear."

"It was nothing," she insisted, more to herself than him. She'd replayed the handful of words exchanged in an everyday, ordinary conversation at the coffeehouse many times and couldn't come up with any quantifiable reason she should be so attracted to Lance. "We didn't even say anything marginally intelligent to one another. We just stared and ogled like a couple of teenagers, right?"

Although, she had to admit, that had been kind of nice. For months, guys had made lewd comments about the catfight. Even guys she'd known and had thought would be above making inappropriate comments had disappointed her, framing icky remarks in the context of a "joke." It'd been a long time since a guy made her feel sweetly self-conscious the way Lance had today.

For a few moments he'd had her wishing she could spend hours hanging out with him. Getting to know every little thing about him.

"You waited by my car in a fake nose to tell me what happened didn't mean anything?" He peered into the rearview mirror and then changed lanes quickly, surprising her with a fast exit off the highway.

"I had a good reason for that." She turned to look behind them and saw a second car swerve onto the exit ramp and nearly hit a city garbage truck. "Has that guy been following us?"

"Ever since the parking garage." Lance navigated the city streets with the ease of a native, finding his way east toward midtown around buses and pedestrians. "I'm taking you to my place so we can talk in private."

The words hung in the air between them like a dare, challenging her to contradict him. How could she get involved with another powerful man whose career would overshadow the fledgling singing venture she'd sidelined for too long even before her divorce?

Worse, how could she allow her crappy claim to fame taint his image and draw all kinds of negative press his way?

"Maybe we should use a run-in with the media to our advantage," she suggested, knowing she'd never be able to articulate her plan once she was alone with him in his apartment. She'd already been dazzled speechless by him once today.

"How so?" He took a sharp left into the tunnel for an underground parking garage, casting them in darkness even though it wasn't quite time for the sun to set yet.

Casting a spell of intimacy in the car that she wasn't ready to feel.

Taking a deep breath, she blurted her idea before she fell captive to the potent attraction between them all over again.

"We need to stage a public breakup."

3

"Isn't it a little premature for a breakup?" Lance steered the car into his parking spot in the subterranean garage and shut off the engine. "We haven't even been to first base yet."

Pocketing the keys, he turned to face her across the shadowy interior. She was incredibly sexy in a short cotton tank dress with a jean jacket thrown over her shoulders. A series of silver pins around the collar glittered even in the darkness, the metal reflecting a light from nearby. She twisted the handle of her leather purse strap between her fingers, her edgy nervousness surprising him. Her reputation painted her as a mouthy rebel. But right now, he never would have guessed she was the same woman who had plowed through the press with an umbrella earlier today.

"And I think it would be better for us if we forgot about first base and um—struck out instead."

"If you had any idea what my on-base percentage is this season, you'd see how unlikely that is." He'd had an epiphany tonight while he was launching that ball into the upper deck. He'd been in the game too long to play it safe. He was at a stage of his career—and his life—where he needed to swing for the fences.

Trying to run his life according to what the fans wanted wasn't going to fly. With his kind of fame, the media could always find something to make him look like the bad guy. He might as well live life to the fullest and hope his good deeds would help show the world he wasn't some shallow playboy racking up the millions for his own gratification.

Now he just hoped he could make Jamie see why that was a better plan. Sure he cared about his career—recognition like going to the All-Star Game and winning a Gold Glove was important. But he'd been playing long enough to know you couldn't live your personal life according to popular opinion. If his fans didn't approve of him dating a controversial socialite, he'd just hope he could provide them with game stats too valuable for the Scrapers to trade him away.

"I'm serious." Her voice turned husky as she pressed the point and something about the smoky quality of it tripped down his spine like a lover's caress. "If we have some kind of public tiff where the media can catch it on film, we can do fast damage control. By the end of the week, we'll be a nonitem as far as the press is concerned."

"Why should we turn our backs on something that might be really special just because it's convenient for my publicist or yours?"

She had no answer for a long moment and he took the opportunity to still her fingers where she wrung the living daylights out of that purse strap. Her short nails had been painted pearly white, the pale glitter standing out against her tanned skin.

He captured one of her hands between both of his, pressing their palms together until he could feel the rapid-fire beat of her heart in the soft pad below her thumb.

"How do you know it could be special when we hardly know each other?" The naked worry in her tone reminded him not to push for too much too fast.

It also hinted at a vulnerability at odds with her brazen public persona.

"I'll tell you exactly how I know, but will you come upstairs with me first?" He gestured to the dark parking garage. "It's quiet in here now, but all it takes is one hungry journalist with a good cover story to get past the gate."

Nodding, she reached for the passenger door handle before he could open it for her. He felt more than a little off his game with her, and he wasn't quite sure why. Could it be because she was the first woman in a long time to interest him on more than just a physical level?

Locking the car, he escorted her to the elevator bay and up to the penthouse level where key access was required. The modest-size high rise overlooked Central Park, an older property he'd been lucky to snap up soon after he moved to the city.

"Wow." Jamie breathed an appreciative sigh as he opened the door to his place, mirroring his own first reaction when he'd seen the view.

The Plaza Hotel capped off the dark expanse of park greenery in the twilight, the brightly lit landmark centered in his glimpse of the midtown skyline. A few hansom cabs worked the perimeter of the park, the colorful carriages a taste of old New York on one of the city's historic thoroughfares.

"Make yourself comfortable." He gestured toward the couch, but she ignored it in favor of a spot at the floor-to-ceiling bay window. "Can I get you a drink?"

"No, thanks." She shook her head, her dark hair spilling over her shoulders to blanket the jean jacket. "But I'm anxious to hear why you think we have any business together when we hardly know each other."

She shot him a rueful grin over one shoulder, her arms crossed in a defensive posture.

Setting his keys on a glass-topped table near the sofa, he joined her at the window overlooking the city. He guessed he didn't have a lot of time to make his case with her. He'd read all about her messy divorce from the media mogul who'd pinned the fault on her in the press. The guy had blamed her partying lifestyle and implied she ran with a "fast" crowd. He'd stopped short of accusing her of cheating on him, but blogs devoted to celebrity-watching had a field day speculating if she'd been as unfaithful to him as he'd been to her.

"I don't blame you for being careful." He respected it, in fact. "From what I read, your ex sounds like he went out of his way to make your life hell."

Though Lance hadn't recognized her at first, he recalled seeing the video of her fight sometime in the past year. It had been in an e-mail a friend sent him, and he'd watched it, the way most of the rest of the country had.

He felt bad about that now, blindly adding to the popularity of a video she surely wished would die.

She gave a tight nod. He was curious why things had turned so bitter in her marriage, but he wasn't about to push her for inside details, the real scoop behind the tabloid scandals. Not when he needed to make her see the past had no business in this discussion.

"And while you might not have any reason to trust that I'm not like that," he forged ahead, "I'll tell you why I trust that we could have something really special together."

She eyed him with wary interest from her position in front of the window. With the skyline spread out behind her, the lights of the city glowing brighter as the sky faded from purple twilight to full darkness, she made for the best view he'd ever had from that balcony.

"Why?" Her crossed arms fell, her body language opening to him for the first time since their exchange in the coffeehouse.

"I make my living on snap judgments, Jamie." With tentative fingers, he brushed a lock of hair from the shoulder of her denim jacket, smoothing it down her back and stirring the clean, floral scent of her shampoo. "I've got fractions of a second to stare down a baseball when it leaves the pitcher's hand to decide if it's a fastball or a changeup or any of the other junk in a pitcher's arsenal. Fractions of a second to apply everything I know about hitting a baseball to determine whether or not I'll swing and where I'm going to try and connect with the ball."

She frowned. "You've made a career out of reading pitches. I don't think you can say the same about women."

His hand lingered on her back, his fingers unwilling to part with the feel of her through the jacket.

She wasn't just beautiful. She was gutsy. Mouthy. Clever. And he wanted her with a keenness he would have never anticipated.

"When I've got a good feeling about something, I trust my gut all the way." He wasn't backing down. "I made up my mind about you."

She shook her head, bemused. "That's how people get hurt. They trust too much, too fast."

He regretted the dark shadow that crossed her expression, the hurt she'd experienced firsthand.

"So don't make a commitment. All I'm asking is for is a night. Just one night together to give it a try." He molded her shoulders in his hands, wanting to haul her close, but wanting even more for her to come willingly. Eagerly. "What have you got to lose?"

A DAMN GOOD QUESTION.

Jamie's knees grew weaker with each passing moment. Lance's touch worked a keen magic on her senses while his crazy approach to having an affair sounded better and better. No doubt it was just because she'd fallen under his spell.

But like he said, what did she have to lose? She was the media's Bad Girl of the moment, the woman most likely to cause a commotion whether she was brawling half-naked or buying her groceries. The media dogged her in the hope of another juicy tidbit. How could it possibly hurt her any more to be with Lance Montero when she was already inextricably linked to him since the video of their meet was posted online?

"I *don't* have anything to lose," she acknowledged, her eyelids falling half-shut under the weight of long-ignored desire. "Not one flipping thing."

And with that realization, a million inhibitions fell away, discarded like yesterday's news. She couldn't come up with any reason why she shouldn't throw herself at the most gorgeous, sexy, sweetly compelling zillionaire she'd ever met.

"One night," she agreed, feeling like the bargain gave her permission to be uninhibited without worrying what tomorrow held. "An outrageous girl like me will try anything once."

Arching up on her toes, she wrapped her arms around his neck and plastered herself—hip to breast—against Lance. It was a bold contact to initiate without so much as a kiss for a prelude and oh, my. Was it ever a brilliant idea. Her body sang with sweet awareness at the feel of all that broad, masculine muscle. From the rugged plane of his taut abs to the sinewy strength of the arms banded around her, he was all about coiled power.

"You're not as outrageous as you pretend." He whispered the words against her ear right before he kissed her just below there.

Delicious chills ran up her spine and she tipped her head back to better enjoy them. Him. This.

"No?" She would go along with anything he said at this point. She just wanted to remain exactly where she was—pressed up against him and on the receiving end of his lips beneath her ear.

"I have a theory that you've got a sweet spot." He cupped her hips and held them to his own, giving her the full, unadulterated preview of what being with him was going to be like.

The hard length of him touched off a fire inside her and she couldn't hold back a gasp.

"See?" He levered back from her to look her into her eyes. "I might have found it already."

Her heart ratcheted up the pace, thundering in her chest with the need for more. She couldn't begin to articulate what she wanted from him. She simply *wanted*.

With frantic fingers, she set to work on the buttons down his shirt. He hadn't worn a tie, but he'd thrown on a jacket with his jeans and dress shirt after the game. She needed them off now.

In her head, she thought about explaining that it had been a long time for her. That her ex had quit caring about sex even before the marriage was over, choosing instead to cheat on her. But her brain couldn't spare enough power to fuel the words past her lips. She was too overwhelmed by the sudden realization that she could have this one night—this one amazing man—for herself. He didn't care about the bad press her behavior had stirred.

That alone made her heart melt.

But the sizzling way he seemed to really, really want her… Well, that had unleashed something primitive inside her that demanded an answer.

"Let me," he told her, stilling her awkward fingers as she battled the last shirt button.

Even her hands hummed with the same fiery anticipation that flickered over her breasts and thighs and everything in between. She felt like an electric current had been turned on, and the effect was both exciting and numbing.

He'd pinned her against the glass window at some point, her back to the view of Central Park and the city so that she could only see the lights reflected in his eyes. She liked her view better.

She watched avidly as he shrugged out of his shirt, revealing a white tank top underneath. She only glimpsed the undershirt for a moment since he gripped the hem and yanked it up and off. Leaving her mouth dry at the sight of his well-honed arms and chiseled chest. A tattoo with his jersey number had been etched on his shoulder. Her gaze sank down the line bisecting his pecs and his abs to end at his belt. She reached for the leather, wanting to see more.

"I can't let you get that far ahead of me." He manacled her wrists with a gentle touch and steered her away from his belt. "First I want to see more of you."

Her inclination was to shimmy out of her jacket and dress in two seconds flat, but he tipped her jaw up to look into her eyes and kissed her.

The warm, silken glide of his tongue over hers undid her. She relinquished control, giving more of her weight to the glass behind her so he could do whatever he wished. Clearly, his ideas for how to proceed were just…better.

The scent of his aftershave called to all her phero-mones, the bay rum seducing her as much as the faint bristle of his freshly shaved jaw. Vaguely, she noticed when he peeled away her denim jacket and smoothed down the straps of her sundress. But mostly, she felt his kiss. He still cradled her jaw like a precious artifact, po-sitioning her where he wanted her for maximum benefit. She'd never felt so treasured, not even by the man whose name she had once shared.

"Lance." She breathed his name like a wish come true, breaking the kiss long enough to revel in the right-ness of the moment.

"Come to my bed." He held her dress around her, keeping her covered. "I don't want anyone but me to see what I uncover next."

The tenderness of that thought undid her. Half the world had seen her breasts, but he wanted to make them for his eyes only, here... Now.

Nodding, she took the fallen straps in her hands and held the dress in place while he led her through a high-tech kitchen into a small study and, finally, a palatial bedroom. A light flickered on at their arrival, treating her to a quick view of a crisp black-and-white domain dominated by an immense mahogany bed.

He dimmed the light with a switch on the wall, narrow-ing the world to the two of them again. Her feet sank into lush carpet as he tugged off her dress to pool at her feet.

She knew a moment's hesitation since her body—her nakedness—had caused so much grief. Would Lance look at her now and think of her past mistakes? But like a balm to her soul, the sight of her in her sheer lace underthings only seemed to inflame Lance. He lifted her up off her feet and hauled her to the bed, depositing her into the thick feather ticking while he shucked his pants.

Excitement coursed through her to be splayed out in front of him in no more than a skimpy strapless bra and matching mauve lace panties, her pulse quickening along with her shallow breath. When he paused to reach into a nightstand—presumably for protection—she couldn't resist touching the formidable bulge in his boxers. Tracing the heavy length of him with her fingertip, she paused at the head of his shaft and encircled it. The shudder that moved through him was visible even in the dim light and she smiled to think she possessed that kind of power over him. Heaven knew he had it over her in spades.

He pressed a condom into her hand, entrusting her to open it as he peeled down her panties. She hadn't even broken the foil when he nipped her breast through the sheer lace of her bra.

"You're beautiful." He tugged the lace down with his teeth, exposing first one nipple and then the other.

She arched up, wanting more of his touch, needing his mouth and his hands everywhere at once. The condom lay forgotten in her fingers until he took it back from her, finishing the job she'd been too distracted to start.

At least, that's what she assumed he did with it. She was too focused on the luscious spasms that seized her when he drew on the taut peak of her breast. The sensation bolted from her chest to circle her womb and clench it hard. Her skin trembled with longing.

He parted her thighs and stepped between them, his expression intense as he watched her with hooded eyes. With restless fingers, she reached up for him, needing to connect with him in some way until the deeper union that awaited them.

He gripped her wrist tight in one hand and guided her

palm to his lips where he kissed it with a fervency that made her quiver. Then, as he kissed her, he aligned himself between her legs and pressed against the slick entrance.

A soft cry escaped her, the pleasure too sharp to contain. Her hips bucked and thrust beneath him, ready for more. Still, he kissed her palm, his tongue stroking an erotic circle along the sensitive center of her hand. The knowing caress could not have been any more effective if he had bestowed the same kiss between her thighs. Tension coiled tight inside, raising gooseflesh all over until she thought she would squeeze right out of her skin.

He never took his eyes off hers as he edged his way deeper inside her, stretching her impossibly while his tongue never ceased the maddening rhythm along her palm.

He seemed to know exactly what that ticklish caress did to her as he increased the speed of it. The touch was so unexpectedly wicked, so sweetly decadent, she had no defense against it.

She flew apart before he even entered her all the way. Her body convulsed around him, and she arched up off the bed in his arms, forcing him closer against her while she came. Release shuddered through her as he pushed his way deep inside her and she'd never felt anything so unbelievably good.

Pulling him down to the bed, she rolled on top of him, needing to have her way with him as she rode the climax through every last lush spasm. Pinning his hands over his head on the bed, she seated herself deep on his shaft. His breath rasped harshly in the soft quiet of the room and she seized on that sound to find the motion that pleased him most. More than anything, she wanted to repay him with the same toe-curling completion he'd given her.

Unhooking her bra with one hand, she tossed it aside

and stretched out over him, brushing her breast against his cheek until he nipped her gently with his teeth. Her hair fell on either side of her, draping them in a silken cocoon as she met his every thrust.

She delighted in her power over him as his hips rose off the bed to meet hers. The sleek athleticism of his body gave her the impression that he could give this to her all night, an idea that sent shivers down her spine. Needing to ensure he reached the peak of pleasure at least a few times, she took up his hand and repaid the torment he'd given her in kind. Tugging one of his fingers into her mouth, she drew on the digit hard. His whole body stilled, and she could feel his pulse pounding between his legs, his shaft rock solid within her.

With light, teasing strokes, she licked along the inside of his finger, and as if she'd flipped a switch, his release roared through him. She sealed his hips to hers, absorbing every thrust.

Afterward, his chest rose and fell with the same panting effort she'd experienced. She lay beside him in the dim light, stroking a lazy finger along his shoulder and up his neck to cradle his cheek.

At first, his eyes remained closed, his expression neutral as he recovered from what they'd shared. But then he turned toward his, eyes opening to watch her. Only then did she understand how completely she'd opened herself to him.

One night?

She had damn well shared more than that with him. She'd might as well have handed him a piece of her heart and soul.

Still, it took several hours and several orgasms more for that reality to sink in. And then, in the quietest hour of the night, she started having a bonafide panic attack at the idea of dragging someone she cared about into her world full of tabloid guerilla warfare and cameras around every corner.

"Lance."

When he didn't answer right away, she shook his shoulder, hating to bother him, but unable to let the knowledge that she'd ruin his career fester longer than necessary.

"Again?" His hand moved on her hip, automatically reaching for her even when he was only half-awake.

Her body responded instantly, and for a fraction of a second, she actually considered the possibility.

"No." Coming to her senses, she edged away from him, dragging a sheet with her as she sat up in his bed.

"What is it?"

"I have to go." She started rooting around the bed for her underwear, thinking maybe she deserved her bad reputation if she would run out on a guy without even kissing him good morning when the sun rose, but damn it, this was for his own good.

"You can't be serious." He sat up, but didn't move to help her find the underwear. Instead, he caught her in midsweep of the bed, pinning her arm to one of the pillows. "It's the middle of the night."

"It's almost dawn," she argued, certain she could see hints of the sunrise through his blinds. "And if I don't get out of here before the sun comes up, the pictures of me doing the Walk of Shame back to my place are going to be all the more disastrous for you."

"Why would I let you walk home?" He looked so appealing with his hair tousled from her fingers and his dark eyebrows pulled in genuine confusion.

Any other man would have seen in a heartbeat that dating her meant trouble.

"Lance, tonight was—" the most memorable night of her life "—a mistake."

"Stop—"

"I mean it. Through no fault of your own, you've got a big, fat target on your chest as far as the press is concerned now that you and I have been seen together multiple times. They will make your life hell even now, but it will be even worse if we continue seeing each other."

Freeing herself, she found her underwear and slid it on. She'd barely gotten into her bra when Lance lifted her off her feet and sat her on the bed again.

"You can't live according to what people expect of you."

"No. But I can make sure I don't detract from what people expect of *you*."

When he didn't argue right away, she guessed he understood her point. She used the moment of silence to find her dress and slip it over her head.

"Jamie."

"Don't." She laid a finger over his lips, quieting whatever he'd been about to say. "I messed up my life with an impulsive mistake. I won't mess up yours with another."

Picking up her jacket, she headed for the door before he could stop her.

"And don't worry," she assured him, trying hard to mold her mouth into an easy grin that didn't feel quite right. "I'll have the doorman call me a cab."

With that, she stepped into the hallway and out of his life, telling herself she'd done the right thing. The best thing for Lance.

She just wished she could have found the courage to walk away from him *before* she'd fallen headfirst for the guy.

4

LANCE SHOULDN'T HAVE BEEN surprised to wake up alone that morning. But he'd gone to sleep with Jamie's scent on his pillow and the memory of her body imprinted on his, so that when his alarm went off, he'd still been disoriented by the empty echo of his bedroom.

As he dressed for batting practice that afternoon, he reminded himself he'd known up front that winning over Jamie would be a long shot after what she'd been through with her ex. When a woman wanted to avoid headlines, the last thing she should do was hook up with a ballplayer. Especially in New York where baseball was more than a hallowed tradition—it was a city obsession when the Scrapers were in the running to make it to the playoffs.

Still, ten hours after waking up solo, Lance didn't want to believe she could turn her back on what they'd shared so easily. The sex hadn't just been recreational. It had been emotional.

Transcendent.

"You look a little misty-eyed, Montero," the first baseman shouted as he tightened the laces on his cleats a few benches away in the locker room. "You're not still reminiscing about that little hopper you hit over the right fielder's head last night, are you? Because if that was as much power as you've got in that bat this season, you'll never beat out a good fielder. Everybody knows Jason Morenz is a game away from going back down to the minors."

The razzing came in fast and furious then. The second basemen took up the cause by reminding Lance he was probably only a year or two away from retirement with such a weak swing and the third basemen contributed run-of-the-mill smears on Lance's all-around shortcomings that would probably knock him out of the running for the Gold Glove this year.

Basically, it was the kind of roast that normally got him going on a slow day, the solid camaraderie that could take a locker room from a bunch of random guys to a committed group that played like a team. Too bad Lance's focus was still on his personal life and the way Jamie had shut down their future together without even giving them a real chance. No option for a dinner date or a movie. Geez, he didn't even have her flipping phone number. Of course, he could find that out no problem— or people he knew could. But would she have a wall of bodyguards around her to keep him away? If so, they'd done a piss-poor job of protecting her from other people out to make trouble for her.

"Maybe Montero didn't see this," called another teammate—a relief pitcher that normally never joined in when the guys got wound up.

Pitchers in general lived on their own planet, coached by a different staff and contributing something totally different than the rest of the players. But when a team had pitchers who would hang with the rest of the guys— that was damn cool and another sign of an organization that could do special things.

"What's that?" Lance hollered back, recognizing the importance of making the pitcher feel like one of them.

The kid was all of twenty-two, weathering a rocky rookie year.

Lance peered through his teammates' shoulders to where DeShea Bronson sat with a Blackberry in hand, his thumbs twitching over the keypad.

"It's the new video your girlfriend posted on YouTube. She's, like, really hot."

Catching the dreamy stare on the kid's face, Lance figured he would overlook the need for team-building if junior got out of line. His jaw flexed as he snagged the handheld device.

"If anyone posted questionable footage of her, I swear I'll find a better use for my bat than—"

The words died on his lips as he pressed the play button.

With ten other guys pushing to get a view of the screen over his shoulder, Lance watched as Jamie lit up the frame with the confident grin he knew hid a more vulnerable woman inside. A woman who had subverted her talents for too long while she weathered one media storm after another.

But she wasn't half-dressed in some grainy video obtained by subterfuge. Thank You, God. Instead, she sat in a seat at a half-empty baseball stadium, the sun streaming down all around her as she adjusted a ridiculous pair of oversize fan sunglasses with the Scrapers logo brightly painted on every conceivable square inch.

She also wore a Scrapers baseball jacket and a team T-shirt tied in a knot just beneath her breasts. Her denim miniskirt looked to have been stuck with team pins up the side seams.

"Greetings, New York!" she trilled out between the snapping of a piece of pink bubble gum. "This is a message to all of you who were kind enough to make my presence felt at Scrapers Stadium last night." She lifted a beer in one hand. "Thank you for cheering Lance on to a three-run homer!"

Lance frowned, confused at what the heck she was doing. She'd made her own video and posted it to support him? How did she think this would throw the media off their scent? Yesterday they'd run from the press. Why would she engage them today unless—

His gut clenched with a new fear.

What if she was going through with her idea of a pubic breakup? She wouldn't really dump him on YouTube. Holy crap, she'd picked a hell of a time to get her confidence back about appearing in public. Apparently just in time to give him the heave-ho like she'd threatened yesterday.

In the video, a small throng of baseball fans clapped in the background, and he could see there were a handful of people seated in the stadium around her only too glad to be a part of a celebrity entourage if just for the afternoon.

"But I want all his fans to know that further imitations of me will not be necessary as I am now a season ticket holder and can be here to support Lance in person." Whoever was working the camera zoomed in on the number of the seat where Jamie was holding court. The camera panned back again, showing the seat's position just above the first-base line.

What was she doing? She'd be mobbed every time she attended a game now that all of America knew where to look for her. Her tactics were a long way from the public breakup he'd been expecting.

"I've got to get out there." He handed the Blackberry back to the pitcher, realizing that Jamie was no doubt sitting in her assigned seat right this very minute. With the Scrapers game not scheduled for another hour and a half, she must have come early for batting practice.

"There's more," the rookie called to him as he headed for the tunnel. "The video still has two minutes to go."

Lance quickened his pace as he reached the passage from the players' locker room to the field.

"That's the problem with you kids today," he shouted over his shoulder. "Too tied to your technology when you could be experiencing real life."

He didn't mind taking time to razz the new guy since his mood had improved ten-fold the moment Jamie said she was there to support him. Hell, she'd essentially announced to the whole world she wanted to be a part of his life. That had to count for something.

Knowing that she wanted to be there for him made his whole season in a way no three-run homer or Gold Glove nod ever could.

Levering open the door into the home team dugout, he stepped out in the sunshine to join the ground crew on the field. Fueled by eagerness to see Jamie, he climbed the rail where the players stood to watch the game and hauled himself up to the roof of the dugout. A small cry went up from a few early-bird fans scattered around the seats.

But his eye went straight to seat 65K, section 22.

Adrenaline pumped through him as his gaze scanned the stadium since he still half-expected her to have meant the video as a stepping stone to the big breakup. But any doubts he harbored fell away as he spotted the big, foam finger she waved that declared the Scrapers were number one.

Grinning ear to ear, he leapt a low concrete wall and sprinted to section 22 faster than he'd ever rounded the bases.

JAMIE HAD PLANNED A SPEECH.

She'd semirehearsed it as a follow-up to her YouTube video in case Lance was nice enough to forgive her for slinking away before dawn after they'd shared the most magical night of her life. That had been a mistake, a knee-jerk reaction to old fears of losing herself in a relationship and not being able to follow her own dreams. But when had Lance ever suggested she be anything but herself? He hadn't seemed frustrated by her outrageousness. The fake nose hadn't rattled him. Neither had her leopard-print umbrella.

In fact, he'd seemed fairly amused at her tactics. All of which helped her to realize she'd been a fool to run away from someone who knew all about her and liked her anyway.

But when she got an eyeful of him in his batting jersey, his number embroidered on the sleeve and the team name stitched across the shirt, all her planned words fell out of her head. The man wasn't just a hot guy. He was a New York icon. And in the hour she'd been in the stadium, she'd been read the riot act four times by different fans who all warned her she'd better not distract "their" shortstop from his phenomenal hitting streak.

She rose from her seat, realizing they had an audience of early fans, but they seemed content to give them a little space. A few sections away, she saw some kids running toward them and guessed that wouldn't last for long.

"So," Lance began, apparently wise to her tongue-tied condition. "I hear you've become a fan of the team."

He eyed her foam finger and she tucked it behind her.

"You saw the video?" She removed her sunglasses and drank in the sight of him without the barrier of lenses covered in trademarks.

"It's been up for twenty minutes and my whole team has seen it. The hit count is already over one million."

She couldn't tell by that answer if he was charmed by her innovation or skeptical of a romantic declaration some might call tacky.

"I thought it was important to show you that I can deal with a high profile relationship." She was grateful to see Lance's teammates take the field for batting practice since their arrival re-routed the swarm of kids carrying balls to be autographed. "After the way I left this morning, I thought you deserved an apology that wasn't just me spouting words—"

"What apology?" He frowned.

Fear tightened inside her. "I thought you said you saw the video?"

She'd worded it all just right in there.

"I left after the first minute or so because I wanted to see you." He reached for her, his expression intent and somehow tender at the same time.

"You missed the apology and you still want to talk to me?" She couldn't believe she would be so lucky to find a man who would let her make such a colossal mistake and not hold it against her.

Hope for a future together unfurled inside her.

"You apologized to me on YouTube." He seemed to weigh the implications of that. "Were you, ah—specific about what you were sorry for?"

"That I snuck out before dawn after you were unselfish enough to give me my first multiple orgasm night?" She shook her head. "I wasn't that explicit, but yes."

At the chorus of gasps nearby, Jamie knew their conversation could be overheard by a smattering of folks in section 22 who possessed sharp ears. But she was past the point of worrying about a public image that had never been stellar anyhow. What mattered to her most was standing right here in front of her and she couldn't risk losing him.

Lance shook his head while one of his teammates teed off on a practice pitch.

"Well, I missed that, but you don't need to apologize for running out." He looped his arm around her shoulders and drew her close. "You'd make me happiest if I could see you in private again, after the game."

Her heart sped up and she felt like she'd just stepped into the sun after too many months of carrying the clouds around with her. Too many months of trying to please mysterious entertainment polls and a fickle public to get a respect that might never come. Being with Lance had helped her see she might as well simply be herself. She had more fun making her video today than she'd had—professionally speaking—in a long time. Being with Lance had opened up a creative door that had been blocked for a while.

"Um—actually, you missed more than just an apology." She hoped he wouldn't mind what she'd posted online. But she'd been following her heart and trying to show him she cared. "I did it out of affection for you."

Possibly the beginnings of love. She could feel the sparkly joy of that emotion underneath all the other happiness, but she wouldn't mind letting that grow as she got to know him. She planned to spend a lot of time in Scrapers Stadium this summer.

"You did what, precisely?" His eyes narrowed, but he still didn't betray any hint of frustration at her quirky ways. Lance appeared curious more than anything. Amused.

"I created a montage of Lance Montero's baseball highlights as a tribute to you, and to prove I'm serious about being a fan." She thought it would entertain his public and show them that she had no intention of distracting their star from his game.

Besides, she was a lyricist. And the funky song had swelled up out of her with practically no effort, as though her music had been just waiting for the right moment to make a comeback.

From down on the field, a familiar tune drifted up to the seats. The voices of at least fifteen guys roused a few of the fans to join in.

"What are they singing?" Lance released her long enough to watch a woman a few seats away as she did a little spin move and hummed.

"I set the tribute to music," she explained. "And actually, I created a dance, too. You know, lots of Super Bowl teams have had their own dances over the years."

Lance clapped a hand over his eyes and groaned, although the sound wasn't completely despairing.

"You know I'm not a contender for the Super Bowl as a baseball player, right?"

"Of course." She'd been really proud of the song, her first stab at being entertaining in too many months. "But you can take a little of the magic that makes football fun to sort of liven up your sport, can't you?"

Down on the field, Jamie noticed two of Lance's teammates yukking it up and slapping their thighs over a shared joke.

"You realize I'm going to get harassed all season for this?"

"I figure you're a big boy, you can handle it." She winked at him and then her smile faded. "But I would feel worse if you didn't accept my apology." She twisted one of the pewter pins bearing the Scrapers logo that she'd used to outline her skirt pocket. "I understand if you can't forgive me, but I did work hard on the montage."

He wrapped her in a bear hug before she finished the sentence, her final word muffled in his shirt.

"Jamie, I want you to ride home with me and never leave." He kissed the top of her head. "Remember? I knew yesterday I was crazy about you. I was just waiting for you to realize we should be together. If your apology means you're going to try to be with me, that makes me the happiest man you can imagine."

She felt the smile in her heart before it reached her lips. Her whole soul seemed to smile.

"Even if your fans think my song is silly?" She hadn't fully thought through that part. She'd just wanted to show him she could handle the public scrutiny, but maybe she'd ended up bringing unwanted attention his way.

"They can sing it all the way to the World Series, sweetheart." He pulled away from her and withdrew her sunglasses from her shirt pocket. "Just root for the home team, and we'll finish this discussion after the game, okay?"

His fans were starting to swarm. The kids carrying clean white baseballs for autographs had returned, and more of the seats nearby were filling up. The ushers in charge of section 22 were starting to have their hands full keeping other ticket holders out of the area.

"Will I get another chance to go back to your place?" She wanted to rewrite the night before. To show him how much a second chance meant.

"Depends." He tugged her down a few rows toward the rail he would have to hop to get back on the field. "You might have to do the umbrella trick to get past the media after the big splash your video made."

She fished in her handbag and pulled out her brand-new Scrapers purse-size model still in the shrink-wrap. "I've got just the thing."

"Then it's a date." He kissed her then, his mouth

settling over hers with warm possession, a kiss that brought out every camera phone in the area and made Jamie's thoughts scramble.

"I'm crazy about you, too," she whispered, keeping the embrace PG out of respect for all the children's charities his foundation helped. She'd studied up on him online and she'd been more than a little impressed. "Swing for the fences, big guy."

His grin wrinkled the corners of his eyes and he backed away to take his place on the field.

"Always."

TALKING SMACK

1

"DON'T STOP."

Javier Velasquez panted the command over a wave of feel-good endorphins as the woman above him sank her fingernails into his inner thigh. He wanted to praise her, to parcel out some kind word to encourage her. But he couldn't even remember her name right now when his body throbbed under her touch.

Sweat rolled down his forehead, a testament to how hard he'd worked himself during the first half of their hour together. But this bliss he felt was more than reward enough. He wanted to kiss his nameless female companion senseless for what she was doing with her strong, silky hands...

"Mr. Velasquez," she said sharply. "Are you resisting?"

The woman was all business when he wanted to revel in the moment. What was it about women that demanded they talk at these times?

"Baby, I can't resist another minute." Opening his eyes, he grinned at her and sat up on the physical therapy table. "Let's ditch this place and go somewhere more private to finish what we've started."

His new athletic trainer straightened from where she'd been working on his groin muscles. The fury in her flushed face couldn't be mistaken and he knew a moment's regret for teasing her. It wasn't her fault his nagging manager had demanded the extra daily sessions with her to prevent another injury this year. He knew these sessions were as much for babysitting purposes as they were for his muscles. If he was in the clubhouse training facility everyday, he couldn't be out raising hell and having fun.

And that's what the Chicago Flames coaching staff objected to about him most of all. They couldn't stand it that their All-Star slugger knew how to have a good time off the field.

"You'd better get your head out of your ass and a muzzle on your mouth, Velasquez." The woman leveled an accusatory finger at his chest as her eyes narrowed. "If you think you can send me running out of here crying sexual harassment because of a few sorry lines I've heard a hundred times, you're sadly mistaken. Now roll over, champ, and take it like a man."

She moved to the sink nearby and washed her hands with brisk, efficient movements, pausing midway to change the radio station from some dentist office Muzak to hard rock. She cranked the volume as if she could tune him out totally, then pumped out massage oil from a dispenser bottle she kept strapped to her waist.

Javier studied her, vaguely disappointed he couldn't coerce her into taking the sweaty session somewhere private. He'd only been half joking about that. The trainer was hot. Even with no makeup and her hair wrenched back in an unforgiving ponytail, she was seriously attractive. The hair swinging against her back was Bond-girl platinum, her figure something any *SI* swimsuit model would be proud to flaunt. She wasn't some overinflated product of Miracle Bras or surgery. She was just perfectly proportioned.

"Well?" She'd turned on him while he was fantasizing about her, and her blue eyes glittered with icy challenge. "Are you going to turn over, Mr. Velasquez, or shall I retrieve the cattle prod?"

"Could you at least call me by my first name if you're going to insult me?" He lay prone as she'd requested, hating the self-indulgent hour spent on his body everyday as if he was some kind of pampered movie star who required a bunch of metrosexual B.S. treatments to appear in public.

Javier had scared off his last athletic trainer by running his mouth and being all-around annoying. In the process, he'd earned himself a week's vacation from the sessions. But his manager had moved quickly to find someone new.

Enter the Bond girl and her almond-scented massage oil that almost drowned out the scent of sweat in the room. She seemed a hell of a lot more immune to talking smack.

"I would do that, but I don't think I can use your first name when you can't be bothered to even *remember* mine after our third session together." She went to work on his hamstrings and he willed away the natural pleasure that touch brought.

He'd had female trainers and physical therapists before, so he knew the drill to keep his thoughts platonic. But today, he didn't feel so inclined to shut down that part of himself. Something about this woman—the facade that said she wasn't backing down—had awakened his interest.

He swore under his breath that they'd gotten off to such a rough start. "If you tell me one more time, I won't forget again, I promise."

If his sleazy pick-up lines hadn't rattled her, he wasn't going down that road again. No sense alienating her totally—especially when her hands kneaded him two inches below the family jewels.

And whoa. Had he thought he could keep his thoughts platonic? Her touch was like a freaking lightning strike to his johnson.

"It's Lisa Whatley." Her dispassionate words reminded him she wasn't feeling him the way he was feeling her.

For that matter, relationships between players and team trainers were strictly off-limits in the Chicago Flames organization, so it was probably just as well that she had discipline. God knew, Javier didn't need to court any more trouble with management or he'd be kissing a fat contract goodbye. He'd pushed his luck with his risk-taking ways this season.

But he'd perfected the art of squeezing every ounce of fun out of life and he wasn't about to stop now. He'd learned to go for the jugular when his older brother—a father figure to Javier—had died young without ever having experienced a fraction of the joys life had to offer. Manuel's self-sacrificing ways had put Javier through school while Manuel had a heart attack at twenty-nine without ever getting to follow his own dreams. Javier had made a mission out of living enough dreams for both of them.

"Right. *Lisa.*" He filed that away in his memory banks and knew he wouldn't forget again. As of today, the trainer had made an impression on him. "If I can't send you running, maybe I can convince you to knock off early once in a while? You know, make both our jobs a little easier?"

The rule against fraternizing with team staffers didn't matter so much if no one knew, right? He debated his chances of spiriting Lisa away from the Flames' headquarters for an afternoon of fun.

She never paused her methodic strokes up his hamstring, the gentle kneading interspersed with light pummeling now that the hard stretches were complete.

"You're trying to corrupt me?" She swapped to his other leg and he lifted his head up off the table to catch a view of her in his peripheral vision.

He saw his mistake right away.

She'd bent forward over the utilitarian bed to reach the far side of his body, the movement highlighting a perfectly shaped rear end and taut thighs all too apparent in her sleek black yoga pants.

The visual that translated to in his mind was of her bent over the table and him standing behind her, exploring those curves with his hands before he plunged deep—

"I wouldn't dream of it." His voice caught on a raspy note as he tried to chase away the image burned in his fevered brain. "Corrupting you, that is."

"Actually—" she finished her massage with a light slap on his thigh before she turned back to the sink. "I think we've worked hard enough today where we could afford to call it quits now."

She ran the water over her hands while Javier wondered how he'd ever get up—er, that is, how he'd ever stand—with her still in the room. His workout shorts wouldn't begin to hide his sudden inability to handle a little physical therapy, something athletes contended with all the time.

What the hell was the matter with him? This woman had gotten under his skin so fast he'd never seen it coming. Most women vied for his notice, attracted to his career and his paycheck. But this one called him on his bad behavior and gave him serious attitude in return. Hell, yes, he liked Ms. Lisa Whatley.

"Does that work for you?" Lisa turned to peer at him over her shoulder as she dried her hands on a paper towel.

Actually, it had all worked a little *too* well for him today.

She had him all wound up and damn near speechless— a condition he was not one bit accustomed to feeling.

"Yeah. Thanks." He wrenched his focus back to a knot in the pine floorboards visible through the hole in the massage table. "I'll see you tomorrow."

When he had his head on straight again and this crazy desire had eased. When he wasn't salivating over her curves and fantasizing about having her in his bed. He hoped she'd grab her bag and go so he could shake off this unwise attraction.

She didn't.

Instead, she dropped onto a low trampoline nearby used for a variety of leg and knee rehab.

"So tell me, Javier," she began, resting her arms on her knees as she shifted into a comfortable position. "Why are you trying to destroy yourself at such an early age?"

LISA WHATLEY WASN'T ABOUT to waste the inroads she'd made with the Chicago Flames All-Star player this afternoon. She'd been hired to do more than administer to the guy's physical well-being. The head of the training staff for the Flames was an old friend and he'd shared his worries about Velasquez's over-the-top behavior.

The slugger had gotten in a motorcycle accident during the off-season and hadn't been wearing a helmet. Then he'd been fined for bungee jumping off a public bridge frequented by thrill seekers. And while no one had ever gotten into legal trouble over the stunt before, the local cops had hoped ticketing Velasquez would serve as an example to others.

Basically, the third baseman had engaged in all kinds of risky behavior, and the team management wanted him to stop. While they could hardly order a psych eval, they could encourage staffers to talk sense into him.

Lisa hadn't promised any miracles, but she had been drawn to the temporary gig because she could identify with that need to live on the edge. She'd been there herself and survived to tell the tale although—heaven knew—it had been touch and go for a while after she'd crashed a prop plane she'd been trying to fly without a license. Walking away from that accident with the chance to reevaluate her choices in life had made her empathize with Javier's situation. She didn't know the reasons behind his risk taking yet, but she identified with him enough that there wasn't a chance she could refuse to work with him.

Javier didn't answer her question for a long moment. Finally, he levered himself up to a sitting position on the table and tugged a fresh towel out of a bin nearby to wrap around his neck.

"Is this for my file, Lisa Whatley?" He clenched an end of the towel in each hand, twisting it. "Because I can go right back to harassing you if you're calling an end to the truce already."

"We have a truce?" She hadn't expected to be even remotely charmed by a man who flirted with danger for fun. After conquering her own daredevil impulses, she'd tended to gravitate toward men with quieter temperaments to reinforce her healthier lifestyle choices.

Yet she found herself wanting to know more about him and not just because of his thrill seeking. After only three days of working with him, she could see his intense commitment to his sport. Sure, he'd made a few asinine comments to her today, but he'd waited until he'd put in his time with her. No whining or excuses about not wanting to perform any of the monotonous and occasionally painful exercises he surely found boring. He obviously took excellent care of himself with or without her, and she admired that kind of physical discipline. She understood better than most people how difficult that was to maintain, especially after an injury like he'd had the previous season.

She'd gone into physical therapy after the grueling months of recovery from her accident. Regaining the use of her leg after the way she'd torn up her hip had been difficult, but she'd been intellectually fascinated by the process enough to launch a career.

"Yes." His dark eyes glittered and she allowed herself a moment to admire his Latin good looks. Tall and dark-skinned, he had pale green eyes that were a surprising combination with the rich color of his skin. His short hair was deep brown, and his features were sharply patrician from the high cheekbones to the straight arrow nose. And as a power hitter, he was strong as an ox, arms full of muscle. "That's what the first-name basis means. I'll stop trying to scare you off, but you cease and desist any attempt to get inside my head."

Her jaw fell open. "I asked you one question. It was direct and straightforward, with no subterfuge." She shrugged her shoulders and stood. "Forgive my curiosity to know what's eating you, but as someone who has dangled at the end of a busted bungee cord and known the merits of cliff diving firsthand, I thought we might have something to talk about besides your lame attempt to pick me up."

Turning on her heel, her gym shoes squeaked on the tile as she marched for the door with a head of steam. He beat her to it. Planting himself between her and the knob before she reached it, her hand connected with his abs instead.

She yanked back her fingers, unwilling to touch him

any more than she had to. Attraction between them would be more than problematic—it would get her fired and could be the final straw in Javier's touchy relationship with the Flames' management. She couldn't afford to get hot and bothered from the sincerity in his eyes or the sizzle in his touch.

"I'm an ass." He held his hands up in surrender, conceding the point. "It's common knowledge around the League. I guess I assumed you'd been briefed on that character flaw."

His hands fell to his sides, but he didn't step away from the door. His quick apology had chased away her irritation anyhow. Ah, who was she kidding? Mouthy Javier had utterly charmed her.

"The character flaw section of the file was too much dense reading, so I skipped it." She didn't plan on letting him get away with anything, suspecting he would steamroll any woman who couldn't hold her own.

But he took no offense, grinning at her in a way that made her heart sit up and take notice.

"That's great. I can start with a clean slate." He reached out to her, surprising her by taking her hand in both of his. "Forget what I said. Forget that I'm notoriously difficult to work with. How about we get out of here and have a drink? Get to know each other in an environment that doesn't involve me being naked or you having a job to do."

Her hand tingled where he touched her. Not like a friendly hum of happiness at being touched, either. This was more like an electric jolt that buzzed with high voltage and singed her in its wake. She yanked her hand back, rattled. She'd touched him plenty of times, so this shouldn't have been a big deal.

But then again, it had been the first time *he'd* touched *her*. The results were skin-tingling.

126 of Sliding into Home

"You know that's unethical for a staff trainer." For a moment, she wondered if this was yet another of his ploys to send her running from this job so he could ditch the mandated workouts in favor of training however he wanted. Or to replace training with activities that were more fun.

Like sky diving.

But Javier didn't seem the type to be anything less than forthright about his motives. Subtlety didn't seem to be a commodity he prized, judging by his recent dust-up with the Boston Aces' catcher, or his ease in confessing to the media where he'd been during the off-season when he took off for the far corners of the world to chase new thrills.

"But you don't work with the whole team, right? You're working with me on a temporary basis. And the coaches aren't going to keep me on a leash forever."

"Do they have you on a leash now?" She couldn't resist the jab since she'd never met anyone less restrained. "From what I hear, you don't answer to anyone. But any way you look at it, I'm an athletic trainer, not a personal trainer. I can't go out for drinks with you."

She shouldered past him, determined not to succumb to the he-man appeal of a guy who lived for the moment. She didn't need that kind of temptation even though she hadn't indulged her adrenaline-seeking side in almost eight years. Maybe it hadn't been such a great idea to put herself in his path in the first place. Who would have thought he could touch an old nerve she'd figured was long dead?

Who'd have thought she could experience such a sharp attraction for a man she'd only just met?

"Wait." He followed her out of the physical therapy area and into the weight room. The Flames' training facility was big and impressive, and she had a long way to walk before she would be home free from the man who'd sent a lightning bolt through her so damn unexpectedly today.

"I can't." She shook her head and kept on moving, not sure if she could outrun the invitation in his sea-glass eyes. "I've got things to do today and I need to—"

He laid a broad palm on her shoulder without gripping it, his touch alone halting her in her tracks. She closed her eyes against the expected jolt and wondered how the hell she'd gone from helping this man to running from him in the course of a brief therapy session.

She was the one who needed therapy, damn it, and not the physical kind.

"Lisa." He turned her around with her name, proving he'd kept his word to remember it this time. "You say you've known the lure of a bungee jump before. How do you feel about something less risky but still fun?"

She had no idea what he was about to suggest, but she was very worried she might say yes. She was a full-time trainer at a local university's athletic department, so she didn't technically *need* the Flames gig. But she cared about her reputation in the industry and wouldn't want to compromise it by making an unwise step with Javier. Still, maybe spending more time with him would give her the insight she needed to understand why he wanted to play with fire all the time.

She just hoped they wouldn't *both* end up getting burned.

"I assure you, I still know how to have fun." She folded her arms to insert a barrier between them, wishing he had a shirt on.

A severe overbite might have helped, too.

"Then how do you feel about kite surfing?"

2

"I CAN'T BELIEVE YOU talked me into this." Lisa strapped on her life vest while Javier checked the lines on her kite's safety harness.

They had pulled into the parking lot at Montrose Beach about an hour ago, and were almost ready for a trial run. The wind was blowing in from just the right direction off Lake Michigan. Other kite boarders were already out on the water, surfing across the waves and catching big air on the major power generated by the traction kites. The sport was similar to windsurfing, but required less wind to generate speed. The gear could easily lift a rider out of the water twenty to thirty feet, a fact which had started to make Javier a little wary.

It was one thing for him to dive headfirst into adrenaline-spiking sports. But was it wrong to coerce his sexy new trainer into something that had the potential to be dangerous? He'd already alerted the lifeguards that she was a newbie and they'd given her a special colored streamer for her rigging to help them keep track of her out in the water. Still…he planned to make sure she stayed safe.

"You think *you* were surprised?" Satisfied that her equipment was ready to roll, he turned his attention to his own. "You could have knocked me over with a feather. It's a rare woman who turns down drinks in favor of kite surfing."

He couldn't deny he'd been thrilled at the time. Before he'd fully recalled how dangerous the sport could be for people who weren't trained. All the more reason to take good care of her.

She didn't look nervous, however. After quizzing him thoroughly on all her equipment, she'd watched a few other fans of the sport on the water and had told him she was ready to be suited up for her first attempt. Now, her eyes glowed with excitement, her cheeks flushed from wind and anticipation as she tested the directional lines that controlled the kite.

"I haven't done anything like this in a long time." She dipped her toes in the sand while her eyes followed the progress of some show-off doing flips and riding his board all the way into the beach—a trick that would get his access card pulled if he wasn't careful. The kites had too much power to be used safely so close to the shore full of people. "I forgot how much I liked the rush."

"A woman after my own heart." Strangely, the sentiment freaked him out when he would have expected the discovery to make him all the more attracted to her. Sure, it was cool to have something in common with the hot, hard-nosed trainer. But she inspired a protective streak he couldn't ever recall feeling on a first date.

"You don't know the half of it," she confessed. "But I'm committed to enjoying the thrill while being safe at the same time. I'm no adrenaline junkie."

Javier wasn't so sure. He'd never met anyone with the same adventurous impulses as him and the knot in his gut made him think he never should have suggested this.

"Let me know if you still feel that way after your first jump." Tugging his board closer to the water, he dragged his safety rigging and his kite behind him. "You ready for a quick lesson?"

Lisa nodded, more eager than she would have ever admitted.

She watched Javier as he took her through the basics of getting the kite in the air even though her fingers twitched on her lines with the need to jump right in and try it herself. Who would have thought she'd end up being drawn in by Javier's adrenaline seeking when she'd planned on helping him find ways to stifle those impulses?

Still, she fully believed she stood a better chance of understanding Javier's need to live on the edge if she ventured deeper into his world, and this day together seemed like a positive first step as long as she could keep a lid on the attraction simmering inside her. Seeing him in a pair of board shorts was enough to make a lesser woman hyperventilate. As it was, she sank deeper into the chilly water whenever he touched her to help douse the fire his fingers could ignite with the sparest of strokes.

Listening to Javier's careful instructions about handling the board and steering the kite, she had to admit he appeared more cautious than she'd been led to believe. He could have boarded out to open water to dazzle her with tricks like the hotshot downwind from them. But he'd taken extra care to be sure she knew what she was doing. And from the counseling she'd received once upon a time, she knew that was a good thing. He placed value on life, unlike the way she used to be.

Willing aside the memories that dark thought inspired, Lisa forced herself into the present, a moment that unexpectedly offered some closure on her long-ago risk taking. Sure, she'd spent years ignoring her daredevil impulses to ensure she had conquered those tendencies. But Javier's invitation had given her a chance to reconcile her old love of high-octane activities with her new, wiser outlook.

"I think I need to just give it a go," she called to him, tugging her equipment deeper into the surf. "I'll be careful."

With remembered skills from surfing, she found it simple enough to get on the board. The trickier part was managing the kite. She fell off a handful of times, dousing herself in Lake Michigan. But seeing the way other enthusiasts managed their lines and took advantage of the wind to cruise along the waves kept her inspired.

"You've got it!" Javier shouted as she finally made it to her feet with the kite in full bloom at the same time.

Her heart lifted in her chest, soaring along with the double foil nylon that pulled on her harness. And pulled.

And wrenched her into the air.

"Aiyeee!" She squealed like a kid on a roller coaster, loving the sensation of the huge kite tugging her up. Her arms burned with the effort to hold on and steer the bar to control where she went. But Mother Nature was no sissy and Lisa quickly realized she had her hands full.

Tucking her knees tight to her chest, she tried to remain as aerodynamic as possible. Even as she soared high above the water, she recognized what a good idea this had been for her. There was a time when she would have maxed out a big air moment for all it was worth, attempting spins or flips to outdo everyone else on the beach. Not now.

Not ever again.

Relief settled over her along with a joyous contentment that she hadn't realized was missing in her life. And she knew just who to thank for it.

JAVIER'S HEART PLUMMETED faster than Lisa's kite.

His throat thick with fear, he imagined a landing that could do extreme damage, knowing he could never reach her in time. Ripping off his safety lines, he detached himself from every piece of gear, not caring if it floated to Canada and back. His arms knifed through the choppy water toward her so he could at least be closer when her board hit the surface.

He would get booted from the beach for getting so close to a kite surfer in flight, but he didn't care since he'd never be able to engage in this sport again if his stupid idea led to her getting hurt.

"Lisa," he shouted up at her, wishing he'd given her more instructions, praying she'd protect herself instead of trying to hold on to that stupid kite.

But as he watched her descent slow, he realized she might have more control of the apparatus than he'd given her credit for. Somehow, the plummet had turned into floating. The nylon kite was moving to catch a slower cross wind, remaining full, but cutting Lisa's speed. Javier waited there, treading water as he watched her board touch the lake, her whole body weight tugging the kite hard to slow herself down. Long, graceful muscles in her arms flexed as she moved, her trainer's body a godsend in the battle with the powerful wind.

Just as Javier realized she would live through the landing and he'd been out of his mind with fear for no reason, he spotted the megawatt grin on her face.

And just like that, his worry morphed to anger, the strong emotions spilling over to his mouth unchecked.

"Just what the hell do you think you're doing?" He reached for her board, steering her toward him before his heart exploded from the strain she'd put it under for the last minute and a half. He felt like he'd just run a marathon, his blood pumping so hard he could feel the vessels jolt behind his eyes.

"I have no idea!" She sounded excited, triumphant.

Oblivious to the scare she'd given him. Her flushed face and bright eyes gave him a hint of what she might look after a night in his bed. "Do you believe I got that high? I've never experienced anything like that."

A few other surfers nearby shouted words of encouragement to her, the streamer from her kite telling people that a newbie had pulled off that sweet landing after the heart-stopping heights she'd reached. Lisa thanked them with breathless enthusiasm as her kite fell into the water behind her. Javier unhooked her lines, needing to return her to dry land before her antics gave him a coronary.

Before her throaty laugh and drenched bikini had him ignoring all the team rules to take her back to his place for a night she wouldn't soon forget.

"We'd better get back to shore before we get booted off the beach." He pulled her on the board, grabbing his gear from a nearby surfer who'd seen his stuff floating out to sea and held on to it for him.

"Did we do anything wrong?" She slipped off her kite board and tried to take it from him, but he held fast to the equipment, unwilling to let her loose in the lake again.

Besides, if he kept his hands full of gear, he couldn't reach for *her*.

"Hell, yes." He looked toward the lifeguard stand, but they didn't seem to be giving the pair of them unwanted attention. "They're strict about making sure newbies are well supervised. You probably gave the staff bigger heart attacks than you gave me. Then I added to the infractions by getting too close to you in flight since I was convinced you were going to crash land."

"Oh." She sounded deflated and he half regretted the gruffness in his voice.

But damn it, he still hadn't recovered from the scare.

"Besides, no sense pushing your luck twice in one

day." He hauled the heavy kites out of the water as they reached the beach and noticed she'd fallen behind.

Actually, as he turned to look for her, he noticed that she'd stopped short at the water's edge, her body dripping wet. She looked like she'd just stepped out of a poster on a teenage kid's wall. Except for the ticked-off expression on her face. Her pin-up's body would turn any guy's head, but he liked to think her bold and ballsy approach to life was something he alone could fully appreciate.

He wondered what it would be like to drag her down to the sand and wrestle around with her, vying physically with the same energy they sparred verbally. Hell, he'd gladly let her be on top for the chance to touch her…

"You've got to be kidding." She shook her head as she continued her forward progress, wringing out her hair with one hand and swiping the other across her face to help dry off. "You're telling *me* not to push my luck? You, who is rumored to have jumped cars on your motorcycle?"

He shook his head to clear it of the image of her wet body astride his.

"I was wearing a helmet that time," he pointed out through gritted teeth.

"You, who once busted your minor league contract by entering a snow motocross event."

"That contract must have been written by a tenth grader it was so damn muddled—"

"And you're the same someone who insists on playing football in a public park every weekend so your coach has no choice but to—"

"Wait a minute." He released all the gear in a pile on the sand and reached for his T-shirt. "I see what you're getting at, and you can't possibly compare that to the scare you just gave me. Playing a pickup game with my nieces and nephews on Sunday isn't the same risk level to me as pulling up thirty feet out of the water was for you just now."

As it was, his pulse still hadn't leveled out. He'd seen her, in his mind's eye, hitting the water wrong or losing control of the board and being hit by that. Or she could have gotten tangled in her safety line, breaking a limb or worse—

He launched for her, wrapping his arms around her without conscious thought. Next thing he knew he was holding her tight against him and breathing in the scent of her wet hair.

"I didn't think about how much that might have freaked you out." Her words were small and far away since he had her locked to his chest.

He loosened his hold just a little, his heart rate finally slowing a fraction now that he had the proof of her well-being in his arms.

"You scared the living hell out of me, lady." He didn't care they were on a crowded beach where people might recognize him. Photograph him.

"Don't you think that's how people in your life must feel all the time?"

It took him a moment to mentally process what she was suggesting. He was so rooted in his own outlook that he had a hard time shutting off that part of his brain enough to consider what it felt like for others to watch him take insane chances.

Damn.

He'd been so convinced he needed to live on the edge to experience every moment and savor the gift of being alive. The gift stolen from his brother, who'd deserved to be married and surrounded by a half dozen kids by now. For years, Javier had been trying to live the dream for both of them.

But was he really doing that? Or was he thumbing his nose at an incredible blessing by risking his life—and at the very least, his career—by seeking new thrills at every turn?

Staring at his brutally honest new trainer, Javier couldn't decide. Feeling like the ground had just fallen out beneath him, he knew he needed to retreat fast.

"I've got to get home."

3

LISA HOPED JAVIER WOULD BE happy to see her.

She'd driven to Cincinnati to speak with him after his game, tired of him canceling their sessions and then using a spate of road games as a way to not see her after what had happened the week before. It hadn't been difficult to find out where the team was staying even though she'd officially quit her duties to the Chicago Flames that morning. She'd hated letting her friend down, but after another restless night's sleep, she'd decided she couldn't harbor feelings for a client, and it had become obvious to her that's what was happening with Javier.

She never would have guessed that such a brief relationship—a relationship that had never even gotten physical—could have such severe consequences for her heart.

But after experiencing Javier's spontaneity and zest for living firsthand, Lisa knew he'd filled a need she'd ignored for too long. He'd pushed her to be daring, and she'd needed that after denying something fundamental in her character. Even though he'd been upset with her at the beach, she'd seen that he'd only been worried. Something she should have simply assuaged instead of challenging him to look at his own daredevil tendencies.

They could be good for each other in so many ways,

and she'd blown it by making their date about issues she should have let him resolve on his own.

Now, seated in the hotel lobby on the Kentucky side of the Ohio River, close to the stadium where the Cincinnati team played, Lisa waited for Javier to return for the night. She hadn't gotten to town in time to see him play, so she'd opted to head straight to the hotel afterward. The players didn't have a curfew even though they had another game the next day, but she'd left a message on Javier's phone earlier that she was in town and wanted to see him.

Would he continue his silence and not show up? She'd been hurt by his retreat and she didn't know how she'd handle a rebuff. The man had dominated her thoughts, dreams, fantasies every minute since she'd last seen him.

A commotion around the front doors distracted her. A handful of people backed into the hotel, holding microphones and cameras all pointed toward a subject who had yet to walk in the door.

Her stomach tightened, knowing who would be the object of this much media attention at an otherwise quiet Kentucky hotel.

"…and I've been friends with Brody Davis ever since." Javier's voice reached her ears before she saw him.

Reporters hung on his word as he retold the story of his truce with the Boston Aces' catcher after an on-field dispute.

Javier wore his street clothes now, but his polished appearance in an expensive suit and starched white shirt open at the collar made Lisa wonder if he had plans for the night. Was she intruding?

She debated turning on her heel before he saw her. What if she'd misread all those undercurrents of attraction she thought were there?

"So you have no hard feelings toward Brody Davis even though he took the first swing that night in Boston?" a young reporter asked Javier as the throng moved deeper into the hotel, the newsman's lips curled with skepticism.

"Davis plays the game the same way I do, and I respect that," Javier told a nearby camera, clearly sensing the opportunity to provide a good sound bite. "He doesn't leave anything on the field."

Pushing out of the crowd, Javier seemed to ignore the next round of questions as he shouldered his way toward the lobby. Toward her.

Nervous anticipation made her heart fluttery and she couldn't decide if it was her "fight or flight" response kicking in—or good old-fashioned sexual chemistry.

As those sea-glass-green eyes locked on hers, however, all confusion dissipated. The urge to launch herself in his arms was so strong it took every ounce of will she possessed to not act on it.

She knew she would look like a deer in headlights in all those photographs the media members were snapping. Frozen. Spellbound by the oncoming collision. But she couldn't do so much as blink to break the spell.

"I know a back way," Javier lowered his voice as he neared her, reaching out a hand to enfold hers. "Come on."

Gladly, Lisa allowed him to take the lead. After just a handful of days without him, she already knew she would follow him wherever he wanted to go.

JAVIER WAS A GONER AS SURELY as the home-run ball he'd blasted over right field in tonight's game. Lisa Whatley had sent his good sense spinning out of control and no amount of time avoiding her would change that.

Not after listening to Lisa's voice in his messages

today, that throaty, sexy tone confiding her need to see him. He'd had time to sort out what had happened between them that day at the beach and knew she'd been balls-on accurate with her assessment of his risk-taking. He just hadn't wanted to hear it.

Now, as he led her to a back service elevator used by the room service staff to deliver food to the hotel patrons, Javier acknowledged that he also hadn't wanted to admit feelings for her. Sure, he'd slept with women faster than this before, but he hadn't had any illusions about where that kind of hookup would lead.

Whereas with Lisa, he'd wanted her more than he'd wanted any other, and the power of that feeling made him hesitate to get involved. He hadn't planned on being tied down during the baseball career he'd worked so hard to develop, wanting to squeeze every pleasure he could out of the dream he'd once shared with his brother.

But Lisa had helped him to see the pleasures he was pursuing weren't really doing jack shit to honor the dream—not his and not Manuel's, either.

But he wasn't ready to tell her any of that yet. He'd put off this meeting so long that by now, he only had one message for Lisa and it required no speaking.

As they reached the fourth floor, Javier tugged her from the elevator and toward his room at the end of the hall. He had a suite that overlooked the Ohio River where he planned to explore this attraction to his trainer in thorough detail.

"Javier." She slowed to a stop beside him as he pulled out a room key.

He peered down the corridor over her head and saw no reporters. They would most likely think he was on the penthouse level anyhow, but the team travel secretary had been helpful in protecting his privacy by securing a room on another floor. Hell, who was he kidding? The team liked hiding him away from the press so he couldn't say anything to cause an uproar.

"I think we got rid of them," he assured her, opening the door to his rooms and ushering her inside.

"I quit the job," she confided, stopping short in the tiny foyer near a slotted bench for removing shoes. "I'm not taking any more contract work for the Flames."

That gave him pause.

"Did I chase you away after all?" He'd been trying to do exactly that when they'd first met since he hadn't wanted the team to tell him how to run his workouts.

But just those few hours spent alone with her had been enough to make him realize he didn't want to do anything to hurt her. He'd get the job back for her if she needed it.

He studied her under the dull light from an overhead fixture, her blond hair gathered in a loose knot at the back of her head with a few pieces slipping free around her ears and neck. She wore a deep blue sleeveless dress that hugged her subtle curves and showcased what a knockout she was. He still couldn't see any makeup on her face save a deep berry stain on her lips. What would they taste like when he finally cashed in on the heat between them?

"No man steers me where I don't want to go," she reminded him, tilting her chin at him with a flash of the bravado she possessed in spades. "I just sensed an impending conflict of interest."

Still, he promised himself he'd look into it to make sure she'd be okay financially without the job. He had the feeling the Flames paycheck was fairly generous. He wanted to make sure she was safe. Taken care of.

And oh, man, he was in deep with this woman, and he hadn't even kissed her. By now, he realized he was falling for her in spite of his best efforts, so why deprive them both of what they wanted—needed—so badly?

"Really?" His eyes wandered down the lines of her body, enjoying the knowledge that soon his hands and his mouth would do the same. "That's odd, because I see our interests aligning quite nicely."

He reached for her, but she sidestepped him with lightning-quick reflexes, moving past him into the room where a bed awaited them. Crisp white sheets had already been turned down.

"If you think that, why have you been dodging me?" She planted her hands on her hips.

He half wondered if she could elude him a second time, now that he was expecting her tricky moves. He admired her athleticism even as he was tempted to test it. This was one chase he would enjoy.

"Looks like you're the one dodging me." He stepped toward her again, but this time, he faked left and moved right, intercepting her neatly. He caught an arm full of silk dress and warm woman. "Or at least, you're trying to."

Squeezing her waist, he reeled her close. The quick move had dislodged a tortoiseshell pin holding her hair in place, and the mass listed precariously to one side until he popped the pin free.

Fragrant locks fell loose as she fixed him with her gaze.

"I'm just trying to figure you out." She splayed both hands on his chest, maintaining a certain amount of distance even as he could see her pulse hammer faster along the vein at her throat.

"And?" He bent close to kiss that throbbing spot at her neck. Her skin smelled like coconut lotion and tasted even better.

"I've got you pegged for a thrill seeker in the bedroom as much as you are outside of it." She arched a pale eyebrow, as if daring him to argue the point.

His heart rate ramped up even faster than hers.

"I think you see what you want because you're a bit of a risk taker yourself." He hadn't forgotten her expression when she came down from the jump on her kite board. "Did you come here tonight looking for a few new thrills?"

She bit her lip, deliberately coy as her gaze slid down and away. Long, dark lashes fanned her cheek as she pretended to mull over the question.

"I don't know about that…"

Ah, this was too rich.

He'd just decided he shouldn't push the envelope so often with his need to live on the edge—and he'd reached that conclusion because of her. Yet here she was, teasing him into temptation.

But maybe this was the better place to seek his thrills. With a woman who was in his life for more than just the fame and the money that came with his career.

"You wicked woman," he chastised her, leaning close to nip her ear. "I might have to teach you a lesson first. It's called, Be Careful What You Wish For."

"You don't scare me, Velasquez." Her fingers slid down the front of his shirt, popping buttons easily as she went. "Did I mention that I only went into athletic training to bolster my passion for the martial arts?"

"I can't wait to find out if you're telling me the truth or if you're just messing with me." With this woman, he wouldn't be surprised either way, and he liked that about her. She was tough and unpredictable, grounded and sexy and forthright. Plus, she was making him hot as hell, pulling his shirt tails out to skim her hands along his waist. "But I'm not going to put that claim to the test right now when I'm most interested in seeing you lose a little of that edge of yours."

He traced the shoulder strap of her dress with one finger, taking a more subtle path to undressing her. When he passed her collarbone, she stilled. At the vee above her breasts, her eyes closed for a long moment.

"I don't know what you're talking about." She swayed on her feet. Her tongue darted out to lick her lips.

"I'm talking about making you hot and breathless and sweetly compliant with everything I want." He parted the fabric of her dress, shifting it off her shoulders until he had to unzip the side to free it the rest of the way. "But first, I'm going to give you a taste of your own medicine."

Her grip tightened on the front placket of his un-buttoned shirt, her hands fisting the cotton as she steadied herself.

"I thought we were thrill seeking?" She didn't sound terribly worried, but the flash of disappointment in her expression amused him mightily.

"You'd be surprised." Tugging her dress down and off, he exposed a navy lace bra and matching panties threaded with a sky-blue ribbon.

A decidedly feminine choice for a woman who liked to appear so no-nonsense on the outside.

"Well?" she asked, sliding a finger under one bra strap as if to continue the unveiling.

He caught the errant finger and pulled her hand, tugging her toward the bed.

"I need some time to appreciate this much of you before I undress the rest." He laid her on the bed and she went willingly enough until he tried to turn her onto her stomach. At her questioning look, he smoothed a palm along her back. "But first I thought I'd give you a little physical therapy so you can see what you put me through that day in the training room."

"That's the taste of my own medicine?" She propped herself on one elbow, one knee drawn up. With her Bond-girl platinum hair cascading down to the bed, she made a jaw-dropping visual. "You want to massage me?"

Lisa watched him through eyelids grown heavy with desire. She had never experienced such a strong urge to pounce on a man, but Javier tested her considerable restraint. Not because he was incredibly good-looking or a stud on the field, but because he was the man who'd called her out of the shadows to embrace her life again.

Although, certainly, the studliness did not go unnoticed. Her hands itched to undress him the rest of the way and see the full impact of his beautiful athlete's body the way God made him.

"You call what you did to me that day a massage?" he asked, pressing her shoulder forward, urging her where he wanted her.

"I'd call it a professional and dispassionate physical stimulation of your muscles." Her heated skin met cool sheets instead of his muscular body and she wondered how she'd sit still through whatever he had in mind. "My job, in other words."

"I'd call it sensual torment." His palm smoothed down her spine to rest at the small of her back, inciting nerve endings far and wide.

She adjusted her cheek deeper into the pillow, taking a deep breath to brace for the sensual onslaught he seemed to have in mind. Pleasure warmed her skin in a full-body flush. Her breasts beaded against the sheets.

"I am a licensed professional," she argued, willing his hand to move. She wanted his touch everywhere at once.

"Hmm." He seemed to consider her words as he

seated himself on the mattress beside her, his hip nudging hers to make himself comfortable. "No wonder your hands felt so damn good."

He skimmed along the band of her panties and traced circles up her back, his touch hypnotically seductive. She debated crawling up into his lap and ending the game by straddling his thighs, but he was so very good at drawing her in. Making her curious.

She wanted to see where it would lead. There was something endlessly compelling about a man who knew exactly what he wanted in bed. Exactly how to please a woman.

"I'm pretty sure I pressed much harder when I massaged you," she offered, stifling the urge to writhe against the mattress.

"You want it harder." His hands slid down her sides, his fingers straying under her arms to cup her breasts. As she requested, he flexed his fingers, increasing the pressure.

"Yessss." She arched back to give him better access, wanting to be closer.

"I see I can't torment you the way you tormented me." He leaned over her, his chest brushing her back. His hands dipped deeper into the lace cups of her bra, baring more. "I want you too much."

He plucked at the taut peaks and she felt the sensuous draw of it all the way to her womb.

"No more massages," she warned, turning on one shoulder to face him. "I can't handle it."

His eyes narrowed in the dim hotel room.

"But I was saving the best massage for last." His hands fell away from her breasts to smooth down her hips and land on the front of her thighs. "I wanted to show you how much I enjoyed those muscle manipulations you performed on the inside thigh."

He squeezed there, the side of one hand rubbing lightly between her legs as he worked the muscle in question. Sensation swamped her, making her quiver from the pleasure.

"You've made your point." She levered herself up to a sitting position and shoved his jacket off his shoulders, taking his unbuttoned shirt along with it. "Now you'd better quit talking smack and start delivering."

She didn't care that she sounded impatient and demanding. She'd been waiting to be alone with him for days.

Fortunately, he seemed ready for more. He angled his shoulders to help her slip off his shirt, his hands only leaving her body for a moment. Then, finally, his mouth met hers in a kiss that sizzled her insides. His tongue played along her lips, but he didn't toy with her for long. His mouth demanded more and she gave it gladly.

Frantically, she worked the clasp of his belt and the buttons of his trousers, her task made more difficult by his straining erection. Or maybe it was so difficult because he slipped off her panties and eased a finger inside her, distracting her hopelessly until he took over the task of undressing himself.

As she lay there, breathless, overwrought and ready for him, she noticed he wasn't wearing that cool, teasing smile anymore. He wanted this as urgently as she did.

Soon, they were both naked and ready, his body a gorgeous sight to behold as he rolled on a condom. The deep tan of his skin seemed to define all his lean muscles, and she couldn't wait to benefit from his strength.

An admiring hum of approval left her lips while she waited for him to come inside her.

Then, he was over top of her, all around her. His

hands hit the bed on either side of the pillow, his knees pushing her thighs apart before he positioned himself right where she wanted him most. She stilled herself for all of two seconds before she wrapped her arms around him, sealing her body to his, breast to chest. He had to alter his hold on her to angle her hips where he wanted them.

And oh. My.

The heat of him stretching her was like no sensation she'd ever known. Javier drew out the sweet shock of his entry, teasing her until she nipped his shoulders and twisted beneath him, then giving her all she could take and more.

Heat roared in her veins and in her womb. The beat of her heart reverberated hard, a grounding force as her nerves wound tight, poised to catapult her into pure pleasure. She grasped his shoulders to steady her, savoring every delicious inch of him as he claimed her. Seduced her body and soul.

Sensation built to impossible heights then spilled over in a climax that shook her very core. She clutched him to her, needing the anchor of his body as wave after wave of bliss undulated through her. For a fleeting moment, she realized he had her right where he'd wanted her all along—breathless and clinging beneath him. But then, he was right there with her, losing control in a climax that followed hers by mere moments.

She kissed his cheek and his neck mindlessly, her face beaded with sweat. His or hers, she didn't know. She only knew she never wanted the night to end.

Because tonight, they were everything to each other. Friends and lovers. Adrenaline junkies who shared a passion for adventure and each other. But tomorrow she'd still be an athletic trainer who worked at a local college back in Chicago and he'd still be an international sports hero committed to his fans 162 games a year during the regular season.

And Lisa was all too aware this was one thrill that might end when the sun rose.

$$4$$

For a man who took a lot of chances with his career and his physical health, Javier recognized he hadn't ever risked much in his relationships.

But now, as he lay beside Lisa in the still hours before dawn, he sensed an unfamiliar certainty in his feelings for the new woman in his life. Their time together hadn't been some casual hookup. Things had gotten intense fast and there could be no going back to simple friendship afterward. He wanted more than that from her.

Perhaps because he wanted to know everything about her, he realized he hadn't shared all that much of himself. He at least owed her some explanation for the other day when he'd run for the hills after kite boarding. He stroked her hair, feeling the soft warmth of her breath against his neck while she shifted beside him.

"So I guess you knew I was freaked out that day at the beach," he began, figuring this counted as a small risk in itself. He hadn't shared the story with anyone else.

"I didn't know if you were more upset because of the scare I gave you or because I suggested—" she hesitated "—that maybe you'd freaked out a few people in your day, too."

"It was a one-two punch, actually. I'd credit both with equal weight. But you couldn't have known why." He shook his head when she tried to apologize. "I was reeling at first because I thought that jump you did was so dangerous and then I saw myself taking the same risks for reasons that once seemed so clear, but now—"

He fell silent, realizing he hadn't started the story in the right place. His chest squeezed tight as he understood that this was going to require more confession. More honesty.

Lisa remained quiet, but she hugged him, her arm pulling tight across his chest as they lay together. He liked the way she seemed to know when to push him and when not to. There was some connection between them he couldn't ever deny.

"My dad was a bit of a deadbeat," he started, remembering all the times Manny had kept Javier on the straight and narrow while their father would drink away any problems for the bargain price of six bucks a bottle. "So my brother stepped up to the plate and raised the rest of us, working when he should have been having fun himself."

He'd never asked for charity. In fact, Javier had busted his hump to bring in money, but just keeping up with living expenses had been tough and Manny wasn't the kind of brother you argued with. He'd had the kind of steely will and work ethic Javier had always admired and Manuel always said his turn would come when Javier made it big in the majors.

"He sounds like a great guy," Lisa observed, her fingers scratching a light rhythm over his skin in the dark.

"He was." It had been seven years since Manny died and the hole inside Javier still hadn't closed. Although, he realized, the cavernous depth didn't yawn quite so wide with Lisa tucked against him. "But he never had his turn to play since a heart attack took him from us before his thirtieth birthday."

Javier felt Lisa wince beside him and she buried her forehead on his shoulder.

"How awful." The simple words summed it up well. "You must have been devastated to lose him."

"I was never much of a risk taker before he died." He'd been a straight arrow, comfortable with Manny's vision of the future and never thinking it might not happen that way. "But afterward, it felt wrong to take any moment for granted, you know? I kept thinking that Manny wouldn't want me to put off any happiness or any pleasure because he'd put off his dreams and got robbed before he could see them through."

"So you've lived the dreams for him?"

"It seemed like the right thing to do." He shrugged, wondering if a shrink would think he was off his rocker. "I never overthought it, I guess. I just felt like all that force and will of his shouldn't die with him. It deserved to be remembered."

A soft kiss landed on his cheek.

"I bet he would be so proud of all you've accomplished."

The words squeezed his heart like a vise—in a good way. Hell, they squeezed so tight he felt the sting of tears. Good thing he was Latin enough not to give a rip that his emotions lived close to the surface.

"Thank you." He swiped a hand across his eyes to chase the burn away. "I was feeling pretty good about it until the other day when we went kite surfing."

She tried to interrupt, but he wouldn't let her, knowing if he didn't finish spitting this out now it could go unsaid for another seven years.

"Isn't it enough that I'm playing in the majors? What the hell would it prove if I break my neck before I'm thirty, too?"

"I didn't know your brother, but I'm willing to guess he wouldn't want you to screw up your career." She rested her chin on his chest, peering up into his eyes.

He could see her clearly now that dawn had broken, the flimsy hotel curtains not nearly heavy enough to keep out the coming day.

She appealed to him in so many ways. From her unflappable, easy acceptance of who he was to her clear-eyed ability to call a spade a spade. He didn't know if he could trust his instincts on a night that had packed such an emotional punch, but he knew he was falling hard and fast for her,

"You're probably right." Framing her face with his hands, he kissed her, rolling her underneath him to claim her all over again.

The peal of his cell phone ring tone shattered the mood.

Although tempted to ignore it, he didn't protest when she thrust the phone in his hand and slipped out from under him.

"I'll go shower," she insisted, picking up her purse and a handful of clothes on her way.

Regretting the loss of her touch, he thumbed the on button after recognizing his agent's number.

His surprise at seeing Scofield's number didn't begin to compare with the shock he felt at the sight of Lisa walking toward the shower. Now that the beginnings of dawn light permeated the curtains, he could see a spider web of intricate markings on her hip, the scars of an old injury he hadn't felt during the night. Scars he hadn't seen that day at the beach since her bathing suit would have covered most of them.

"Javier?" his agent's voice called him out of his brooding thoughts.

"Yeah, I'm kind of busy right now." He planned to

confront Lisa with all haste to find out what those scars were. Were they from her old thrill-seeking days?

"Have you seen the morning news?"

Javier checked the bedside clock.

"It's not even seven."

"Somebody dug up the dirt on your trainer girl-friend." Scofield didn't sound pleased and Javier tensed, wondering what beef anyone could have with Lisa. "And I don't think the Flames are going to appreciate you dating someone who is as much of a head case as you."

LISA WARBLED HER WAY through an old show tune as she rinsed the last of the hotel conditioner from her hair. She was in the process of enjoying the sting of hot water on her back for an extra decadent moment when the stream stopped short. Blinking fast, she discovered Javier in the shower beside her, his arm bracing the curtain open while he cut off her spray.

"I hope you're going to make that up to me—" Her words halted as she spied the expression on his face. At once blank and forbidding, he stared at her with the dispassionate regard of a stranger. "What's wrong?"

"Apparently we made the morning news." He handed her a towel even though his gaze never slipped south of her eyes for a second. "Someone snagged a photo of us at the beach last week and I can only guess they sat on it so they could do a little investigative reporting to maximize the value of the picture."

Lisa's skin chilled. Her heart hitched for a moment at the disappointment—anger—in his eyes.

She wrapped the towel around her and sidestepped him in the steamy bathroom.

"And?" She could only imagine what an investigation into her past would bring.

"And you nearly died in a plane wreck eight years ago." He placed his hand on her hip, clearly having seen the scars on her leg from that very same accident. "While I don't give a damn what my manager has to say about me having a relationship with a woman who lives on the edge as much as me, I definitely give a damn that it never occurred to you to tell me—"

"You knew I had a similar past." Feeling defensive, she reached for a second towel for her hair. Had she lost any chance they might have had at a relationship by not confiding in him?

"But I didn't know it had almost killed you."

His words burned a hole in her heart, making her wonder why she'd withheld that piece of her past even after he'd opened up to her about his brother. They had found something special together, but if they weren't careful, they could hurt each other in the end.

She might have already hurt his career irrevocably, in fact. She'd taken her job with the Flames to try and help him past that need to take risks, but instead, she'd allowed herself to be caught up in the irrepressible hunger for life she saw in his eyes. Now, the chances the Flames management would send him packing had increased ten-fold because of her.

"It made me stronger in the end." She pulled away, worried their time together might be drawing to a close and unable to think how to salvage a relationship without hurting each other more. "I shattered my hip and had to relearn how to walk. But it made me appreciate every second. I learned to appreciate my own worth."

"Why didn't you tell me?" He studied her as if he'd never seen her before and she realized maybe he hadn't. Javier had been so forthright about who he was and what he wanted from life, but she'd grown more guarded than that. She wasn't used to baring her secrets. Exposing herself and her fears.

"I have a hard time—" She cleared her throat and wondered how she would walk away from someone who truly understood her and cared about her. His tender concern made her eyes burn for what they might have shared. But how could she allow him to sacrifice his place on the Flames for her sake? "Listen, maybe it would be best if I go."

He did a double take that was so overt it would have been cartoonishly funny if it hadn't been a heart-wrenchingly awful moment.

"Leave? You want to leave after what we shared?"

Guilt pinched her, but not as much as the guilt she knew she would feel if he got booted off the team because of her.

"Do you really want to lose out on your baseball career after all your brother's sacrifices?"

He shook his head. "My God, Lisa. You can't seriously hold that over my head."

The tears behind her eyes built until they threatened to spill over at the slightest movement.

"I'm sorry. I just can't imagine that you'd be happy without the career that's meant so much to you. It's one thing to walk away from the risk taking, but it's another to walk away from baseball." Just saying the words aloud reassured her it was the right thing to do to leave. "You're too talented for that, Javier. You deserve a place in the stat books and a long, lucrative career that will entertain fans for years to come. I would never want to give your team a reason to release you after how hard you've worked to get here."

He watched her for a long moment before he shook his head. The stark look in his eyes cut her to the quick.

"When we met, it was me who was trying to send you running and now that I've succeeded, it's the last thing I want."

"I never meant for this to happen," she assured him, swallowing past the lump in her throat. She reached for her clothes near the bathroom door. "Goodbye, Javier."

Closing the door between them, she dressed quietly and left the room, knowing she'd never seek him out again.

5

LISA DIDN'T TAKE ANY satisfaction from the hitting slump Javier fell into after she left him that day.

His slugging percentage took a nosedive over the next five games, a fact that was front page news in the *Tribune*'s sports section after their last home game. Not that she was obsessed with the man who got away or anything. Javier's stats were just common public knowledge since Chitown loved its sports heroes.

A love she was afraid she might share.

In the last week, her heart had experienced a worse pain than that prop plane crash eight years ago. She had renewed understanding for what it felt like to be broken and vulnerable, except these hurts were all on the inside, too deep for any therapy she knew.

She entered the Flames' training facility on an off-day, knowing the team was traveling for a road game the next afternoon. She'd been putting off the chore of cleaning out a small locker at the center, not wanting to run into Javier after the way things had ended between them.

Thankfully, interest in her had died down when the media failed to snag any other photos of the two of them together. The Flames had come out in support of Javier despite the earlier insinuations in the press that Lisa was a daredevil who wanted to lead him even further astray. The flap had ended after a few days and she'd wondered if she'd been overcautious to take the allegations so seriously.

Since then, her former supervisor had asked her to come in for an exit interview and to pick up her things, and he'd been glad to let her do the first over the phone and the latter during off-hours since the Flames wanted to low-key her involvement with the team after the news coverage. She'd turn in her key before she left today and then her last tie to the sexy third basemen would be broken.

It felt odd to be in the training facility alone. Some of the staff traveled with the team and those who didn't had already left for the day. She passed a door for the club house and tried not to think about Javier.

"Lisa."

A man spoke her name from the shadows of what she thought was an empty conference room and she yelped in surprise.

Slowing her step to see who was inside, she saw a heart-achingly familiar silhouette.

Javier.

"I didn't think you'd be here," she said, realizing too late how revealing that statement must be. Since when did she sneak around trying to avoid someone just because he had the power to break her heart? Straightening, she ignored her galloping heart rate and walked on. "Excuse me," she murmured.

"Wait." He stepped out into the carpeted hall behind her, his tall frame flanked by historic posters advertising old games. "I've been trying to see you."

He tucked his hand around her elbow lightly enough, but it was a touch she felt in every fiber of her being. She hoped he didn't feel the small, bittersweet shiver that trembled through her on contact.

"I don't think that's such a good idea." She'd be throwing herself at him in no time.

"I shouldn't have let you have the last word the other day." He gave her a rueful grin. "That's truly unlike me and it should tell you how much I value your opinion."

She clutched her building keys tighter in her fist, needing to exit the conversation before her heart melted like ice cream at the ballpark.

"I appreciate that, but—"

"But you were dead wrong." He silenced her with his words, calling the shots in a way that made her smile despite her misery.

"How do you figure?" She avoided his eyes, staring instead at the whiteboard where the trainers scheduled the therapy rooms ahead of time. She noticed her old schedule with Javier had been erased, though no one else had taken the slots with him.

"We shouldn't end this." He reached for her shoulders, approaching her slowly, giving her time to object.

She remained silent, longing for something she had told herself all week she couldn't have.

"We belong together, Lisa." His hands landed gently on her shoulders. "Before you left to take a shower that morning, I was already making plans for taking you sailing and diving. Then when that phone call came about our pictures in the press and your past—" He clutched his chest. "I was just caught so damn off guard."

Seeing this big, strong man hold on to his heart like it was a fragile thing warmed her insides like no amount of words could have.

"I should have told you about the accident—"

"No." He shook his head. "You would have told me in your own time. Being in the spotlight the way I am— it puts my life under the microscope and forces things onto center stage that don't necessarily deserve to be there. I think the only reason I let you leave that day was my own fear that we're so alike that you'd hate living in a fish bowl in the long run as much as I do so maybe us being apart was for the best."

She tried to follow his train of thought, confused but liking the direction of the words very, very much. A spark flared over the ashes she'd been stomping for nearly two weeks.

"Still, I should have told you about the accident. It was important." As much as she had practically swooned at the chance to touch him and feel his gorgeous body all over hers, she knew now they should have spent more time talking first. "But everything happened so fast that night."

"I was in a hurry to be with you."

The warm rasp of his voice told her that he had the same delectable memories of that night that she did.

It would be so easy to step right back in his arms…

"But maybe falling into bed wasn't a good idea for us." She didn't want to make the same mistakes with him. Not after how much it hurt the first time.

"No. It was the best idea ever." He sounded so damn sure of himself. So arrogant. So oddly charming.

She couldn't help a grin. "How do you figure?"

"I found out how wildly passionate I am about you." He said it the way only a Latin man could—as if he was swearing a vow, as if his life depended on the words. "If I didn't know that, I probably would have just slipped out of that hotel room the next day and gone on with my life, none the wiser that I might be walking out on the most amazing woman I'd ever met."

Javier held his breath, hoping his words would penetrate the cool veneer Lisa had worn from the moment she'd spied him in the conference room tonight. He'd been begging the training staff to get her back here for days, needing to see her in person to straighten out the mess they'd made of their relationship. To make his case for a future.

But it wasn't until tonight that she'd agreed. He'd probably be fined if he didn't find a way to get to that game tomorrow, but if it took all night to convince Lisa he was worth a second chance, he'd gladly pay the fine.

And right now, he wasn't sure if he was making any headway on that front. She wasn't easy to read, even in the harsh office lighting outside the training staff room.

"I don't want to—" she made a vague gesture between the two of them "—melt all over you again."

The breathless quality of her voice made him wonder if that was a real possibility. He never would have guessed it from her straight shoulders or her tilted, defiant chin.

"Even if I made it *very* worth your while?" He didn't touch her, but he stepped closer. Close enough to breathe in the clean scent of her shampoo. The crisp fragrance of her perfume.

Her eyes dilated, but she shook her head.

"If we talk instead of—" she made that vague gesture again "—jumping into bed for the second time, we might understand each other a lot better."

That meant there was the possibility of jumping into bed in their future. His heart lightened.

Determined to do whatever was necessary to reach that point—not just because of the sex but because of what it would mean to Lisa—he squared his shoulders and prepared himself.

"Then we will talk." He kept his voice low in deference to one of the janitors pushing a mop cart.

The building was quiet, but not deserted.

"*Talk* is not a dirty word, you know." Turning, she used one of her keys to open the door to the staff room. Letting him in, she shut the door behind her and he found himself in an area he'd never seen. Lockers on the wall were interspersed with health-related posters and life-size diagrams of various knee and ankle injuries.

"Too bad." He sat down on one of the benches near the small lockers. "I might like it better if it was. But what should we discuss?"

If he had a topic, he could start tackling it. The sooner he could assuage her concerns, the sooner she'd be back in his arms where she belonged.

Lisa spun a combination lock and opened the metal box before withdrawing an extra T-shirt and a bottle of hand lotion.

"For starters, you never asked me about why I took such risks." She pulled out a hikers' guide to the Rockies and he wondered if she was going on a trip he didn't know about.

Maybe talking wasn't a bad idea.

"Did you lose someone close to you, too?" Could she have toyed with living on the edge for similar reasons as him?

"No. I did it for attention at first. My mother was an addict and it took a lot to get her attention. Later, I did it to feel alive since sometimes I felt damn invisible in my house."

"Ah, damn, Lisa. I'm so sorry—"

"No." She waved a rolled-up weightlifting guide under his nose. "I've made peace with all that. I just wanted you to know that's why I've avoided thrill seeking for years. It felt too much like an addiction. But being with you made me realize I wasn't always acting out. There was a lot of escape and genuine joy in pushing the limit. I'm athletic and coordinated, healthy and smart. Why shouldn't I be as active as I want to be?"

Alarm pricked along his nerves.

"As long as you're careful." He couldn't keep his hands off her anymore, needing to feel her against him. "Okay?"

He'd begun to appreciate how much he had to lose if he wasn't more cautious in life, and he hoped she felt the same.

He rose to wrap her in his arms and thanked God that he had found her before he took one too many foolish chances with his life. He felt like he'd awoken from a long sleep since meeting her.

She nodded against his chest, her fingers smoothing the fabric of his T-shirt along his shoulders. Warmth filled him along with all that same fierce possessiveness he'd experienced that night in his hotel, only this time, he knew he wouldn't succumb to wayward fears that she wasn't as she seemed.

He knew better. His tough, Bond-girl trainer was a straight shooter. A sexy, vibrant woman. And she spent her free time planning hikes in the Rockies.

He couldn't believe his good fortune.

"Javier?"

"Mmm?" He kissed the top of her head and wondered if he could talk her into making good use of that massage table.

"I heard something about you being in a hitting slump."

It took a moment for the comment to sink in.

"Are you asking about this as my trainer or my girl-friend?"

"I'm not your trainer anymore, remember?"

"I hope to lobby for a few very private sessions." Thoughts of the massage table returned. "But since it's my girlfriend asking, I can tell you confidentially that I'm in a slump because I've been craving sexual satisfaction."

He felt a shiver pulse over her skin and he smiled to think he had that effect on her. Heaven help him, he would not take it for granted.

"Don't you dare try to play me, Velasquez. I think I'd better critique your swing before your game tomorrow. Shouldn't you be with your team tonight, by the way?"

She blinked up at him, her eyes accusing even though her mouth remained soft and open, ready for his kiss.

He slipped his hands beneath her blouse to caress her bare skin.

"When the head trainer told me he thought he'd finally convinced you to come into the office tonight, I damn well wasn't going to miss the chance to see you."

The days he'd waited felt like weeks.

"How are you going to get to St. Louis in time for the game?"

"Depends how long it takes me to convince you to come with me." He kissed her lips, tugging on the soft fullness of the lower one for a long moment before he released her. "If it's soon, I'll drive down. If you require a lot of persuading, I can try to pull together a charter flight."

She swayed toward him, dropping her weight-lifting guide as she wrapped her arms about his neck.

"Hmm. How persuasive can you be?"

"You're looking at the next Gold Glove winner, sweetheart, and they only give those things to guys with very good hands…"

THE LAST INNING

1

TONIGHT, RICK WARREN wasn't going to be leaving the locker room. Delaney Blair would make sure of it.

She stood just inside the empty administrative offices of the Atlanta Rebels' clubhouse, a mere few yards from where Rick sat in the nearly vacant locker room. Her fingers shook a little as she tightened the tie on her sarong and then fluffed the silken tails of the knot to fall between her breasts. She'd dressed carefully—or rather, undressed—for this night when she could find him alone.

Rick was frequently the last to leave the locker room anyhow. A fact she knew because she'd been paying close attention to the Rebels' first basemen since he'd joined the team her father owned. Delaney had never been all that interested in her father's organization while she'd been growing up, her overriding idea of baseball players being that they were overpaid and thought highly of themselves. But since Rick had come to town, Delaney had to revise that opinion.

She peeked out through the blinds in the front office to watch Rick as he joked around with the cleaning crew. Six foot two with golden-brown eyes and longish dark hair that made him easy to pick out even in his ball cap, Rick was the quiet sort around his team. A loner. But he always had time to ask the woman who gathered the dirty uniforms about her two sons in college or razz the guy who ran the floor washer about being a die-hard New York Scrapers fan.

One of many things that made Rick Warren worthy of the risk she planned to take tonight.

Carefully closing the gap in the blinds before anyone noticed her spying, Delaney waited for the cleaners to vacate the locker room. Rick liked to avoid the press at all costs, so he always took his time leaving the clubhouse after a home game. The press had started paying more attention to him this season, speculating about what he'd do now that his two-year contract would be expiring with the Rebels.

That damn contract had forced her to brash action tonight. Well, that and a recent bit of news that had inspired her to take life by the horns.

She'd wanted to catch Rick's eye for months. His habit of keeping his head down and his MP3 player cranked up around the clubhouse made that difficult, however. Add to that her own natural shyness and she figured the two of them would never move past the occasional lingering glances across a crowd.

That would change tonight. As she peered out once more between the gap in the blinds, she noticed the big bins of dirty uniforms were gone and Rick was alone. He sat on a bench between his locker and Dwight Wrigley's, his baseball cap on backward as he clicked the controls on the MP3 player.

Luckily, it didn't matter how loud he had the tunes cranked in his ears. Taking a deep breath, Delaney checked the knot on her bright green silk sarong and slipped into her fuchsia high-heel mules. The vivid colors made her feel a little more strong and confident when she was scared inside. She'd never done anything drastic to make a man notice her. Never put herself on the line so completely.

But a cancer scare could light a fire under anyone. And after waiting for tests on a lump that had turned out benign, Delaney didn't plan to wait anymore. Starting tonight, she was going after what she wanted.

Drawing open the door of the administrative offices that led into the locker room, Delaney eyed the man who'd captured her attention with his head-down, plow-through-anything work ethic.

"Rick?"

She said his name even though she knew he wouldn't hear her with the ear buds in. Still, he must have sensed someone else in the room because he looked up.

Their eyes met. Locked. And reaching for the knot of silk just above her breasts, she loosened the tie.

Her sarong fluttered to the floor like a drowsy butterfly as Delaney bared the new, bolder woman who wouldn't take no for an answer.

THERE WERE SOME THINGS in life a man couldn't tune out.

The roar of thirty-thousand fans during the play-offs. The flash of police lights in the rearview mirror. And a nearly naked woman prancing purposely into his line of vision.

Somewhere in Rick Warren's head, a voice told him to run and get a towel for her to cover up with. To throw his team jacket around her shoulders. But since he'd seen her untie her little scarf dress with his own eyes, clearly she'd intended for this show to happen. A show involving no clothes except for sheer lace and satin panties that matched her strapless bra.

"Ms. Blair."

He might have stammered when he said it. God knew, his thoughts were stammered. Stumbling.

Could a player be released prematurely from his

contract for seeing the owner's daughter naked? Maybe he'd be sent to the minors. Hell, an ultraconservative owner like Daniel Blair III would set up a Single A team in Siberia just to punish Rick for an offense like this.

That kind of penalty had crossed his mind in the past any time Rick had thought about acting on his attraction to the quiet beauty he'd had his eye on ever since setting foot in Atlanta.

Her lips moved, but Rick couldn't hear what she was saying, calling to mind the ear buds he still wore. He tugged them out with one hand and chucked the electronic device into his open locker behind him, his eyes never leaving the golden skin of the goddess strutting his way.

A fantasy come true.

"Call me Delaney." She smiled at him with a Mona Lisa lift of her full lips.

He'd heard Delaney Blair was adopted, her features Eurasian exotic. The long sheet of straight, dark hair gleamed with good health. Her eyes tilted up at the corners, but her generous height and bronze skin suggested a wide range of ethnic forbears. No matter her origins, she was a sight to behold even with her clothes on.

And *now*... He sucked in a long breath in an effort to drag in enough oxygen to clear his head. No dice.

"Ms.—ah—Delaney. I shouldn't have stayed so late." He thought about standing and realized his veins might not have enough blood flow available to fuel his legs for that kind of movement.

The wholly unexpected striptease had had immediate physical consequences.

"I've been trying to capture your attention all season." The smoldering temptress paused in front of him, hooking her thumb in the waist band of her barely there underwear. "Every other time I've attempted to get to know you better, you've found an excuse to bail."

His gaze went to her thumb as it tracked the band of white ribbon threading through the panties.

Through the erotic fog that enveloped his brain, he recalled Delaney looking his way a few times at a meet and greet early last season. At the time, he'd been too new to the club to know the lay of the land and he hadn't wanted to start off his tenure with the Rebels as the guy who tried to schmooze the owner's daughter.

And then, the longer he'd been with the club, the more convinced he became that dating one of the Rebels' most prominent team attorneys was a bad idea. She worked for the organization he played for. Hell, she was the one who'd signed his damn contract. Rick had always walked the straight and narrow and he didn't think now was the time to start veering from the path, especially when he'd finally landed on a team that could reward his years of loyal service with a championship.

"I'm no good at small talk," he hedged, a little shell-shocked that this woman would be in here with him alone right now, peeling off her clothes.

As Daniel Blair's daughter, Delaney was strictly off-limits. Cool and aloof, she was always at the fringes of every team gathering with the top brass. Which, per-haps, accounted for why he'd crossed her path at the oc-casional party. He tended to hang out on the sidelines a good deal himself.

Once he'd noticed her that first time, he'd looked for her at every team function, admiring the way she carried herself. Of course, he'd never seen her carry herself quite this way.

"Me neither," she agreed readily, taking two steps

closer. Putting one creamy thigh within touching distance. "Which is why I opted for a more obvious overture."

"Maybe we should talk about this with your clothes back on?" He turned to check the door, needing to be sure there were no witnesses. "I'm pretty sure I could get traded for this. Or worse."

He needed to get her dressed and out of here before his career imploded.

Her mouth compressed into a flat line and he wondered how often the beautiful owner's daughter had encountered obstacles in her life.

"Is a scantily clad woman throwing herself at you such a common occurrence that you don't think twice about ending the moment?" She fisted a hand and planted it on her hip.

Damn. He didn't want to offend her any more than he wanted to be caught in a compromising position. Forcing himself to stand, he reached behind him to retrieve a clean jersey from his locker.

"Hardly." He tossed the jersey around her shoulders, his number 11 curving around her breasts. "Is having your own way a common occurrence for you?"

After draping the shirt from his road uniform over her shoulders, he found himself trapped within man-snaring range of her perfume.

"I've rarely thought about what it means to have my own way, let alone gone after it, actually." She tilted her head sideways, considering. That long, dark sheet of her hair slipped down her arm with the movement, baring the side of her neck.

She made the admission so softly, her words so full of honesty, that he regretted giving her a hard time. He knew damn well she was the most unselfish woman in the world. She spent her weekends at charity functions, using the team's name and visibility to rake in donations for good causes. She had gone to work for her old man at the Rebels' front office at an early age and probably made only half as much dough as she could if she'd taken a gig in finance and international law, both of which she had degrees in.

Ah, damn. He knew way too much about her.

The sudden flood of pink in her cheeks made him curse his total lack of manners. Why embarrass the hell out of her when she'd only been making a brave bid for his attention? God knew, he didn't look up from his own path in life very often to notice what the rest of the world was doing. What right did he have to judge her motives?

She turned. "If you'd rather I go—"

"Wait." He took her shoulders in his hands, putting her right back where she'd been. He wasn't sure what else to say now that he had her attention.

But just about then, his brain started broadcasting updates on all the ways his body wished to capitalize on this moment. She'd taken a huge risk to grab what she wanted. And he couldn't deny that he wanted her, too. So how could he possibly ignore her sweetly perfumed skin, her long lean limbs that his shirt did nothing to cover? The swell of cleavage that distorted the number on his jersey lured his attention back to her breasts.

And hell, yeah, he knew he was making excuses to follow his libido, but he was also quickly losing the will to give a damn.

"Nobody's twisting your arm," she said, her voice little more than a whisper as he tried to make sense of what was happening.

He'd seen her, noticed her in the way a man notices a woman, and yet he hadn't acted on that in the year and a half he'd been here because he'd tried to throw all his focus on his job.

No more. A shot at a championship wasn't worth throwing away the chance to touch her.

Delaney Blair had bared more than her body to him just now. She'd bared her desires. Her hopes. And she was—without a doubt—the sexiest thing he'd ever seen.

Bracketing her hips, he quit thinking and drew her close. Her gasp of surprise fanned the latent heat in his chest.

And he kissed her.

Gently, he brushed his mouth over hers, savoring the soft swell of her plump lips. She tasted like cinnamon— hot and sweet at the same time. Intrigued, he caught her jaw in one hand and held her steady as he conducted further investigation. Her lips were coated with something slick and sweet. But as good as she tasted, her lips weren't enough a moment later. Heat flared all over his skin, firing his blood and igniting his hunger. Her body brushed up against his as she shifted position—a knee here, a thigh there—communicating tantalizing hints about how good it would feel to have all of her pressed tight to him.

He forgot who started this, forgot anything but the need to have more of her. Anchoring her with a hand splayed against the small of her narrow back, he teased her lips apart for a deeper exploration. She opened to him on a sweet, audible sigh of pleasure, an enticing sound he made it his mission in life to hear again.

Driven by a rush of hot desire, he backed her up a step and then reversed their positions. Guiding her through the break in the benches, he situated her against his locker, needing his hands free.

Heat crawled up the back of his neck, making his

freshly showered skin itch with impatience to have more of her. His fingers speared beneath the jersey he'd covered her with, greedy to map every inch of unfamiliar terrain even though he knew every second he touched her was bringing him closer to the point of no return.

"You should stop me," he warned her, certain he could rein it in on her command, but not entirely sure that he could still accomplish the feat on his own.

He'd had himself on a tight leash for the last two years, determined to finally achieve the elusive career goal of a series title in Atlanta. What if he'd used up all the restraint he possessed in those two years and he didn't have enough to let go of Delaney?

"I don't want to stop," she assured him, her fingers working the buttons on his shirt with slow precision.

His thumb brushed the underside of her breast and she made that sweet sound again, the one he'd hear in his dreams tonight and every other night.

"You deserve more. Better." He knew that in his rational mind, but that didn't stop his one hand going to work on the clasp of her bra while the other slipped beneath the underwire to cup the soft, full weight.

Her teeth clenched as she hitched in a breath, her back arching to increase the friction of their bodies.

"I deserve *this*. Just exactly this."

He rolled one hardened peak between his thumb and forefinger, knowing he was lost to this. To her. If she wasn't going to say no, he didn't have a prayer.

Just then, a flash of light filled the room.

Delaney let out a cry of alarm. What the hell?

Rick turned to see what was happening, wondering if someone from the cleaning crew had returned. But there was no mop cart or floor cleaner inside. Just a brief glimpse of a tall, skinny guy with a camera.

"Hey!" Rick shouted, unable to go throttle the guy without letting go of the half-naked woman in his arms and exposing her to the intruder.

"It's okay." Delaney wriggled free of him. "I'm fine. Go get him."

Needing no more encouragement, Rick sprinted toward the spy, but the son of a bitch was right next to the emergency exit near the stairs. Calling on the speed that made him a stealing threat on base, Rick jumped a bench between him and the door and took off up the stairs.

If he didn't catch this guy, there would be hell to pay when his picture appeared in the paper with a half-naked Delaney pinned against the lockers. Her father was going to love that.

Rick would be out of Atlanta before tomorrow night's game.

Turning the corner to take another flight of stairs, he heard a car start in the distance. In the employee parking lot. Spinning around, he went back to the previous landing and plowed through the heavy metal door in time to see a car burn rubber on its way out of the lot.

Cursing a blue streak, he knew he was screwed. And not in the good way.

No wonder he'd kept his head down and his nose clean for two years with the Rebels. The one time he gave himself permission to enjoy life, it bit him on the ass with a surefire ticket off the team.

But even as the curtains threatened to fall on his career, Rick turned to jog back down the stairs to Delaney. If he was going to be lambasted publicly for his indiscretion, he would damn well have the satisfaction of seeing their encounter through to completion.

2

THERE WAS SOMETHING foreboding about Rick's footsteps on the stairs.

Delaney heard it as she retrieved the sarong from the floor and retreated back to the main office to find more substantial clothing. She needed to speak to someone on the building staff about tightening up security at night, but her thoughts were too scattered to follow through on the task now.

She'd made a play for Rick and it had backfired with flare. Now she owed it to him to do the damage control it would take to protect his position with the Rebels. No doubt about it, her father would have him shipped to Seattle or Arizona—somewhere far from here—even if he had to trade for less talent. Her daddy might accept that he couldn't interfere in her life anymore, but he'd have no qualms about interfering with someone else's if he thought he was protecting her.

Damn it.

She adored her family, but they had never thought twice about meddling in her affairs. Some days she still wondered if it had been a bad decision to work for her father since it put her very much within his reach if he chose to stick his nose in her business. But the work was fun and exciting, a family legacy she was as proud of as any other Blair.

"Delaney." Rick's deep voice sliced right through her churning panic, putting all her focus back on him.

A shiver tickled her skin as a parade of sweet, sensual memories reminded her how exhilarating it had felt to be in this man's arms after fantasizing about him for too long.

She looked up to find him in the doorway between the locker room and the reception area of the front offices.

"He got out of the building?" She was already unlocking her office, needing access to her computer if she wanted any hope of spinning the story. "Any chance you recognized him from press conferences? If we can figure out who he works for—"

"A guy like that wouldn't be at a press conference. Anyone snapping those kinds of pics isn't a member of the legitimate media." He followed her into her office, his shirt still half-buttoned from her roaming fingers.

Wow. She couldn't help a moment to admire the view since she wasn't going to be able to capitalize on it tonight. Rick needed her help now.

"I'm so sorry I put you in such an awkward position." She shouldn't feel embarrassed—that had been the whole point of her disrobing tonight. But she was confused and worried and still extremely turned on.

Being a selective dater had left her without a man in her life for almost two years—a fact that coincided neatly with Rick's arrival in town. And frankly, doing without for two years made a woman—edgy.

"What awkward position?" He shrugged. "I had my clothes on and I was standing in front of you so no one will know you were undressed. The way I see it, those photos are going to cause the kind of public flap that keeps sports stars in the papers. It's not always a bad thing."

While her brain grappled to comprehend how he

could think this wasn't a crisis in the extreme, he turned to close her office door. Then he locked them inside.

She jumped at the sound of the lock catching.

"What are you doing?" She clicked through a few keys on the computer, hoping for inspiration on how to handle this situation. She'd worry about beefing up security tomorrow. Tonight, she needed to help Rick prepare for a media tsunami.

"I'm making sure lightning doesn't strike twice." He stalked toward her.

He couldn't be suggesting what she thought. And then it occurred to her what he meant.

"You want to be sure there are no more unwanted intruders." How crappy that they had to think that way in the heart of a building owned by one of the best bankrolled teams in baseball. "But I don't think our picture taker would be stupid enough to come back here tonight."

She moved to take a seat at her desk. He moved faster. Planting himself in the leather chair, he was already there when she ended up in his lap.

"Good." He gathered her legs in his arm and spun her so she sat crosswise on his thighs. "We can finish what we started."

The thrill of delicious possibility tickled her skin.

But she could not let it sweep her away again. She'd been so damn close to exactly what she'd wanted and instead she'd ended up with a publicity nightmare on her hands.

"No." She had to close her eyes when she said it. She couldn't have refused that hot look in his eyes otherwise. Not after she'd dreamed about Rick looking at her this way for so very long. "I need to salvage this before those photos show up somewhere and—"

"Why?" He ran one hand up her thigh, his touch

impeded by such a thin layer of silk she could feel every nuance of his palm through the fabric. "The damage is done. We might as well wrest every ounce of pleasure out of this night if we're going to pay the price for it tomorrow."

His fingers began to bunch the sarong in his palm, lifting it higher on her thigh with each clench of his fist. She had to squeeze her thighs tight to stifle the stir of liquid heat between her legs.

"But the damage hasn't been done." Levering herself upright, her hip grazed the evidence of his desire straining the fly of his khakis. She could have cried with the frustration she felt at having to ignore it. "I can't let you suffer the consequences of bad press and my father's retribution if there's any chance we can buy those pictures or halt the story."

"I'm a grown man. I make my own choices and I take full responsibility for my actions." His level look dared her to challenge him. He kept his arms around her hips, holding her there.

"I know." Her heart beat faster at his declaration, further proof that he was an honorable man worthy of her trust. "And while I admire that about you tremendously, the truth is I caught you off guard by stripping down in the locker room and effectively instigated the whole thing because—"

She stopped herself just in time. Yet, judging by the narrowing of his gaze, her save hadn't been timely at all.

"Because why?"

She took a deep breath, inhaling the scent of lemon oil on the freshly polished office furniture and a hint of spicy aftershave.

"Because I've had a bit of a crush on you for a long time." It was true. It just wasn't the whole truth. So she braved a little more. "Because I was afraid you'd leave at the end of the season without me ever getting to know you and I—didn't want to wait for life to happen to me anymore."

She watched him, hoping that would be enough for him to release her, to let her go to work on fixing the mess she'd made. Given a little time, she knew she could find that rogue photographer. The pool of sleazy journalists in Atlanta was small and the pool of folks who would cover baseball stars was even smaller.

"Why now?" Rick asked, as if he'd telepathically keyed in on that one kernel of information she'd hoped to keep quiet. "Why tonight?"

The temptation to fib came and went in about a nano-second. She'd gone into contract law because she'd known she'd never be a litigator. It just wasn't in her nature to lie, especially not to a man with the kind of upstanding values that made her notice him from day one. Rick Warren was the go-to player on the team when you needed a base hit or to advance a runner. An unselfish player, he did his job year in and year out whether or not he got the spotlight or the fattest contracts. And she admired the heck out of him.

Her tongue darted out to moisten lips gone suddenly dry. Bracing herself, she revealed the truth.

"I had a cancer scare."

The clock ticking on the wall above her office desk reverberated through the room like it was counting down the seconds until doomsday.

"Are you okay?" He unlocked his hold on her hips to grip her shoulders, squaring her body to his as if to take the news head-on.

She nodded, her throat suddenly tight with the memory of all the fears and scenarios that had gone through her head two weeks earlier when she'd been terrified that a doctor might tell her she had a finite time left.

"I'm fine." She released a shaky breath. "Wonderfully, gratefully fine. There was a lump—" she gestured toward her breast where a tiny stitch remained "—but it was benign. Just a scare that had me up at night thinking about what I'd do differently if—"

Her throat closed up again.

He rubbed her shoulder, a touch of comfort that turned sensual when he laid his palm on her neck and stroked her cheek with slow sweeps of his thumb.

"I like what you did differently."

Her eyes locked on his, searching for clues that he was teasing her.

"Not just because you took off your clothes." He shifted their weight in her leather office chair, tipping back so that she had no choice but to lean into him. Her head came to rest on his shoulder, her ear close enough to his heart to feel its steady beat. "Although that was great, too. But I'm glad you put yourself in my path tonight. I noticed you as soon as I was traded to the team, but I put you out of my mind because of who you are."

"The owner's daughter." She recognized the conflict of interest there. "I didn't think it was a good idea in theory, either. But on those sleepless nights when I had too much time to think…I didn't care about that."

Rick let her words flow over him as he held her, knowing there was a message in there for him, too.

She thought *she'd* been playing it safe on life's sidelines for too long?

He'd walked around the Rebels' clubhouse for two years with his headphones on and his focus on baseball, never resorting to the showboating crap the younger players used to make a name for themselves with the fans or the media. He wasn't hitting the weights every day or chugging protein like water in an effort to hit one out every at bat. Most of the big sluggers would never think of a sac fly or batting around the bases.

And while Rick was proud of the kind of ball he'd played during his ten years in the majors, he sometimes wondered if he shouldn't draw a little more attention to himself. Not because he wanted the glory. But what if the next generation of players in the game were only hearing about power hitters and home runs? If the strategists didn't step up now and then to talk about the finer points of winning, the league might not attract the kind of guys it took to round out a team.

Yeah, Rick could very much appreciate the need to do things differently. To step out of the safe zone into the spotlight even if it wasn't comfortable.

"I don't care about the fallout from this." He rejigged her weight on his lap, seized with a sense of purpose where both she and his career were concerned. The new position put them eye to eye again. "I don't want to spend another second thinking about some sleazy photographer or what might happen tomorrow."

"I can't allow you to be traded because of me."

"I want you to let me handle this." He had a plan and he'd figure out how to implement it tomorrow. "For now, I'd just like to help you celebrate your good news. Your good health."

She shook her head, ready to argue. He kissed her to press his point. He didn't stop until she softened against him, her body boneless as she molded herself to him.

"I must be crazy," she whispered, when he finally broke the kiss.

"No. You're just living on your own terms, remember?" His heart slugged hard against his chest, his adrenaline cranked at the thought of being with her. Seeing her burst into the dark locker room in her bright colors tonight had been like someone turned on a light switch in his head. "Are you okay with this?"

He skimmed his fingers along the top of the sarong and tugged gently on one end of the knot.

She swayed toward him.

"You're very convincing." Her eyelids fluttered and closed by a fraction.

"So are you." He pulled the end of the fabric and unfastened the knot, unveiling the lemon-yellow bra he'd glimpsed earlier and releasing a hint of her scent. "The sarong almost gave me a coronary when you strolled into the locker room in that thing."

She placed a hand on his heart.

"How about now?"

"Do your worst." He could feel his pulse spike at her attention, his blood rushing through his veins with the heat of knowing he'd have her soon. "I'm all yours."

He wrapped her tight in his arms, fitting her curves to the aching heat of him. Any reservation he'd had about this in the locker room had incinerated, leaving only desire and possessiveness for this shy, sharp woman who could have any man she wanted and chose him.

Unbelievable.

Capturing her mouth with his, he kissed her hard. She tasted so sweet he couldn't possibly get enough. Not in just one night. But that didn't stop him from exploring the slick, smooth surface of her teeth or the velvet glide of her tongue at length.

The temperature in the office flared hotter than a sauna. His skin pricked with a primal need to clear her desk with the sweep of his arm and take her here. Now. Instead, he lifted her out of the chair, standing with her in his arms to cross the dimly lit room where a long, low couch awaited. Her computer and a small desk lamp cast a bluish glow around them as they fell onto the sofa, her back cradled in his arm when they dropped into the cushions.

He levered back enough to look at her. She made a mouth-watering picture, her eyes glazed with passion and her lips red and plump from his kisses. Her silky dark hair fanned out around her shoulders, an inky-black background for the brightly colored undergarments he couldn't wait to take off.

"I would like a better look, too," Delaney whispered, her hand moving to his belt buckle. "You have a few fantasies to live up to, you know."

With a roll of his shoulders, he had his shirt off since the buttons had been undone earlier.

"Is that right?" The thought of her fantasizing about him singed any restraint he might have had. "I like the idea of you lying in your bed thinking about me."

He unfastened his fly and stepped out of his pants. Her eyes never left his body, her gaze following his every move.

"I'm glad I can do more than just think about you this time." She reached for the waistband of his boxers, one shiny red nail dipping below the black cotton elastic.

He stopped her, unsure how much foreplay he could withstand given the long drought in his sex life. He'd barely dated in the last two years. There'd been a couple of girls in all that time, but they'd been mutually casual hookups that had barely taken the edge off.

"I'm going to be honest. I'll need to be inside you about two seconds after you touch me, so maybe we should make plans for protection first." He had nothing with him since he'd had no reason in the world to guess the sensual feast he'd walk into today when he arrived at work.

"You didn't feel this earlier?" She reached into her bra and withdrew a foil packet from the left cup. "I didn't have a pocket, so I was forced to work with what I had."

"Very resourceful." He took the condom and laid it on the coffee table before pushing the glass-topped piece aside. Kneeling beside her, he positioned himself near her hips. "I've got a few hidden surprises myself."

He saw her eyes widen as he bent to kiss the patch of satin that covered her mound. And then he didn't see anything else, his world narrowed to the scent and taste of her as he kissed her intimately.

Delaney gasped at the feel of his tongue taking shocking liberties with her. She'd never—well, she'd just *never*. Even her one long-term relationship had been more cerebral, the sex more restrained. But *oh*. The way Rick touched her, kissed her, was exquisite.

She heard her own harsh cries, but was powerless to contain them as he swept aside her panties for better access. She considered protesting for the space of a heartbeat, but then she remembered her original quest for the night.

No more tiptoeing around the fringes of life. She planned to dive right in.

And as Rick laved every inch of her with languorous kisses interspersed with strong strokes, she knew she wasn't on the edge anymore. He'd thrust her into the eye of a sensual hurricane, her nerves overwrought and swirling with raw sensations that threatened to drown her in a blissful delirium.

Her head thrashed from side to side, as if she contended with some darkly sensual force within. But whatever the encroaching feeling was, it seemed determined to have her way with her. She tried to be still, to let it happen and let Rick do as he wished with her body but—

"Oooh!" The climax hit with the force of an oncoming freight train, rocking her body at its very core with lush spasms.

Her fingers sank into his shoulders, holding on for dear life as he gave her the first man-induced orgasm of her life. She could scarcely catch her breath in the aftermath, the residual shockwaves blindsiding her even after he released her to undress them the rest of the way.

"I've never—" She shook her head, at a loss for words. Licking her lips, she started again. "Let's just say, you have far better tools at your disposal than me."

"Glad to hear it." He'd rolled on the condom at some point. Now, he positioned himself between her thighs. "That means you'll have to come back if you want more."

"I'm ready for more right now." Still trembling from her release, she rubbed herself shamelessly against him.

He obliged, entering her by slow, heart-stopping degrees. Her back arching, she wrapped her legs about his hips, sealing them together.

He supported her spine with one arm, his fingers tunneling into the back of her hair to hold her steady for his kiss. With his deft mouth, he reminded her subtly of the pleasure he'd provided her moments ago in that most intimate of places. The slide of his lips on hers became all the more erotic, all the more intoxicating to her overloaded senses.

The pressure built inside her, both from being impossibly stretched and from her own mounting pleasure. He found a rhythm that sent her reeling, the glide of their bodies a seamless union.

Vaguely she wondered if a woman had ever fainted during sex. Lights flashed behind her eyes and a sweet light-headedness made her cling all the tighter to him. Next time she would cater to the man's every carnal desire. But right now, all she could do was hold on and ride the wave as another orgasm seized her. She cried out as her heels dug into his back, her hips tilted to meet his fully.

In some part of her mind, she recognized that he found his release, as well. He throbbed inside of her, his shout echoing hers. Delaney couldn't remember any moment in her life ever feeling this perfect. As they rolled to lie on their sides on the sofa, their hearts pressed so close together that the beats seemed to fall into synch.

Right then, she couldn't work up the least bit of regret about their night together. Frankly, she couldn't imagine any consequence that would make her think this time with Rick hadn't been worth it.

Still, if he got traded tomorrow because of her—because she'd put a good, upstanding man in a compromising position—she didn't know how she would handle it. She'd never anticipated that living life to the fullest would mean the heartache would be every bit as potent as the pleasure.

Unwilling to let those thoughts overshadow this one night, Delaney released her hold on Rick enough to plant a kiss on his chest. And then another, lower down.

If she was going to go through life with this night imprinted on her memory, she planned to make sure he couldn't forget her, either.

3

FLASHBULBS POPPED in Rick's eyes as he adjusted the microphone at a podium in a midtown Atlanta hotel.

Eager journalists raised their hands all over the ballroom while others shouted out questions at the hastily assembled press conference.

"Rick," one of the loudest voices called, "you've got to admit the woman in this photo bears a strong resemblance to owner Dan Blair's daughter—"

"I've got no comment on that," Rick repeated for the second time, shutting down the question posed by the Rebels' beat writer for the ATLANTA CONSTITUTION JOURNAL.

Rick had called a press conference first thing to respond to the photos that had appeared on a celebrity magazine's Web site and then innumerable fan blogs.

While the traditional media hadn't run the pictures that hardly counted as "sports news," reporters from those same media outlets had phoned the Rebels' front office for comments on the photos.

Rick had barely left Delaney's side that morning when he'd started getting calls from his agent, his manager and even a couple of teammates who said they were only looking out for him. Rick had given himself just enough time to run home, shower and change before meeting with an independent publicist. He didn't have his own media person and he sure as hell wasn't going through the team publicity guy, so it had seemed the best course.

He'd avoided the media for most of his career, and look how far it had gotten him. While he never would have been the kind of guy to kiss and tell after a night with a woman, the photos told their story whether he wanted them to or not. And since that was the case, he would put himself in the media spotlight this once to deflect attention from Delaney and keep the focus on him.

"You expect us to believe that anyone but a Rebels insider would have access to the locker room on a game day?" a skeptic piped up from the middle of the pack, her tone both condescending and chiding.

"Hey, one of you guys managed to worm your way into the locker room on a game day," he pointed out, pausing for a sip of water from the bottle under the podium. "It's not exactly Fort Knox over there."

That brought a few chuckles of appreciation from the crowd. Clearly the press corps was well aware of how low some of its more smarmy members would stoop.

"Have you been summoned to the front office yet, Rick?" someone else called out, and he recognized one of the staffers for a big sports radio affiliate.

No doubt those guys would have a field day with this story. Sex and scandal sold papers and increased audiences better than home runs. It was one of the reasons Rick wasn't exactly a household name despite ten seasons of solid defense, consistent RBIs and not a single appearance on the disabled list.

"No." Rick wasn't looking forward to the inevitable talk with management given how much he wanted to remain in Atlanta. The Rebels finally had a shot at the series this year, and if not this year, they'd be there next year for sure. The last thing he wanted was to be traded off a team that might finally make it to the big dance. "And you know as well I do that this unfortunate invasion of my privacy is my personal affair and not team business, so I don't anticipate having to defend myself to the team."

He signaled to the P.R. consultant that he was done and pushed back from the podium, confident he'd done what he could to steer interest toward his career. He'd downloaded his stats from the Rebels' Web site and had them passed out as people came in to remind the reporters he was all about baseball.

Although, truth be told, he'd never realized how unbalanced that might have made his life until Delaney strode onto the scene.

"Rick," another voice called after him before he left the small stage. "Can you at least tell us if you've ever met Delaney Blair?"

The crowd quieted as they'd all heard the query, too—and were every bit as eager to know the answer.

Never had it grated more to know he could generate ten times the interest in his career by selling out his personal life. Guys did it all the time by dating high-profile women. And while Delaney wasn't a movie star or a pop singer, she was a member of a family that was practically baseball royalty. The Rebels had been family owned since the franchise's beginning, carefully preserving their status as majority shareholders even after the team went public.

"The Blairs are an Atlanta institution because they make it a point to personally greet every new player to the organization." He glared at the throng of reporters scribbling furiously, his gaze skipping over the cameras recording his every word to focus on the faces. "They have my utmost respect."

The partitioned ballroom erupted with more questions, but Rick walked off the stage and through a side exit into a food prep area. Even the busboys were lined up to watch the press conference, their water pitchers and cleaning rags idle in their hands as Rick plowed past them into the bowels of the hotel's kitchen.

He didn't need to stay for the rest of the event. He was footing the bill after all, and he'd had his say. But as his cell phone chimed in his jeans pocket, he acknowledged that a lot of other folks would feel like they hadn't gotten theirs.

Checking the caller ID only out of morbid curiosity, Rick saw a set of digits he couldn't ignore. "Blair, Daniel" wouldn't make a call from a personal line just to shoot the breeze.

Rick might fool a few people by hedging around the identity of the woman in the photograph with him, but he damn well wouldn't fool her old man.

Knowing the time had come to face the consequences of his actions, Rick answered the call to find out just how badly he'd screwed up his career. He didn't want to leave Atlanta, but he'd be damned if he would compromise the team or Delaney by staying in a situation that would only hurt them all in the end.

"YOU CAN'T BE SERIOUS."

Delaney paced the floor in her father's luxurious home office at the family compound in Buckhead. She'd been summoned in no uncertain terms just past dawn, when her ringing cell phone both awakened her and alerted her to Rick's departure sometime while she'd been sleeping.

His silent exit had stung, leaving her unsure of all the feelings he'd stirred the night before.

"I assure you, Laney Lou," her father used the old family nickname for her. He picked up a silver-framed photo of her as a baby and stared at it as if he was talking to the round-faced infant instead of his grown daughter. "I am most definitely serious about wanting your young man to do right by you."

Oh, sweet, merciful heaven.

"Dad." She crossed the Persian carpet in the big, octagonal conservatory that served as her father's home office. Every wall that wasn't a window or a bookshelf was covered with cherry wainscoting. Vintage baseball memorabilia dotted the shelves along with his collection of Irish wolfhound statuary. His two flesh and blood dogs rose to their feet as Delaney neared their master. "This isn't the 1950s. There is no quantifiable 'right thing' to be done after a man and a woman share a kiss."

"Is that what you call it these days?" Replacing the photo in its frame, Daniel Blair III turned his laser-blue eyes to settle on her at last. He had a powerful aura about him despite his five-foot-six frame, and he'd always been the source of hero worship for her from her earliest memories. He'd given her a pony for her tenth birthday. But he'd also given her a liberal education abroad, including stints in desperately poor countries so that she knew better than to take her blessings for granted.

"Excuse me?" She halted her progress, reaching out to pet the dog closer to her in the hope she could at least win over one of the males in the room.

"This." He waved a printout of the photo snapped of her and Rick in the locker room. "Is this what you call a kiss?"

Her cheeks burned. Could this be any more awkward?

"I really don't think anyone has the right to judge a private moment but the parties involved."

One of her father's shaggy gray eyebrows lifted.

"This isn't one of your legal documents. This is my first basemen." He brought the paper up for a closer inspection. "Are you even wearing clothes in this photo?"

She slapped a hand over her eyes.

"Dad, I'm a twenty-eight-year-old woman." Still, there was something about being interrogated by the family patriarch in the heart of his lair that made her feel like she was sixteen and in trouble for staying out too late after the dance. "I wouldn't even be here right now discussing this with you if I hadn't wanted to make sure that Rick isn't penalized in any way for what happened."

Her heart did a funny double-time beat at the mention of his name. He'd never been far from her thoughts today, and not because of the stupid photo leak.

No, she'd been thinking of the way it felt to drift off to sleep in Rick's arms, her head pillowed on his bicep and her leg tucked between his.

"What makes you think you'll fare any better?" Her father tossed the printout on his massive desk and then folded his arms over his gray, worsted wool vest. "Don't forget who you work for, miss. As far as I can tell, you should both be penalized for conducting your private affairs in the workplace."

"So fire me." Indignation burned away any residual embarrassment. She was excellent at her job as a contract lawyer and her services came damn cheap since she was family. "Maybe free agency will be a good thing for me. But don't hurt the team by trading away one of the most productive first basemen we've ever had."

Her father studied her for a long moment, and she wondered if perhaps she'd gotten her point across. But then his eyes narrowed and he lowered his voice.

"Has it ever occurred to you maybe he wants to get

traded and this is precisely the sort of stunt that he knew would send him on his way?"

Just the idea of it gave her a physical jolt. But she knew Rick better than that.

"Don't be ridiculous. He's going to be a free agent after the end of the season. He doesn't need to resort to underhanded tactics to get out of the organization."

Did her father believe she was naive enough to fall for that kind of manipulation anyway? Of course he did. He knew as well as anyone how little she'd dated. Half the reason for her selectivity had to do with the man in front of her. She loved her dad, but he was a tough critic. Having him doubt her judgment now made the ache in her chest all the worse.

He leaned back to have a seat on his desk. Folding his arms, he toyed with one silver cufflink, spinning the emblem around and around.

"The boy wants a spot in the playoffs," he reminded her, bringing to mind the buzz about Rick even before he joined the Rebels. After having spent the first eight years of his career as a utility player bounced around the league, Rick had made noises about wanting a shot with a team who could make it to the playoffs.

Worry knotted in her chest. It was one thing for her father to toss out a ludicrous suggestion during an emotional argument because he was worried about her. But it was another for him to have thought about the notion enough to actually be concerned how he presented it to her. That meant the full wisdom of megasuccessful Daniel Blair III had been applied to the equation and he still thought Rick Warren might have orchestrated some elaborate setup to pave his way to another team in the league.

"But the Rebels are over five hundred." It was a stronger position than they'd been in the last several seasons after the All-Star break. "He can have the shot at the playoffs here."

"Sure," her father agreed, nodding while he continued to flip around the cufflink. "But he'd have a better chance in New York or Boston."

The truth of his assessment sent her back a step. Sure, she'd been the one to make the overture toward Rick. But could he have capitalized on the moment for reasons all his own? No, no, and hell, no. This was simply what her father did—plant enough doubt to make her second-guess herself. But it wasn't happening this time.

Behind her father, the intercom buzzed on his desk, followed by his secretary's voice.

"Mr. Blair, Rick Warren is here to see you."

The news of his arrival felt like confirmation of her fears. Why would Rick be at her family's home so soon after the story broke? Could he be here for the kind of closed-door meeting that got players shipped out in record time? Had her father even summoned him, or had Rick arrived to do some negotiating of his own?

"Send him in please," her father said, before turning to her. "Perhaps we'll be able to decipher the young man's motives sooner rather than later."

She'd barely blinked away her surprise when Rick charged into the room without being announced, her father's personal secretary hurrying in behind him to apologize for the intrusion. With a flick of a weary wrist, Daniel Blair waved away the employee while Rick looked back and forth between Delaney and her father.

"I want the first flight out of here before this mess snowballs any more."

4

RICK HAD BEEN PREPARED for Delaney to argue with him. She'd made it clear he shouldn't have to leave the team because of this.

But he hadn't expected the color to wash out of her cheeks before a fiery flush took over. If he didn't know better, he would think she was furious. Her old man had invited him out to the house to hash through this today, but now Rick wondered if the team owner had set him up for a big fall. Certainly Dan Blair didn't jump in to defend Rick even though the guy had been reasonable enough on the phone. He'd told Rick he was sure he'd do the right thing as far as this scandal was concerned.

From what Rick could tell, that meant removing himself from the equation to squash interest in those pictures and to protect Delaney. Once Rick left the team, there'd be no more lurid speculation about what happened. The media would be too busy dissecting how he fit into a new roster. As for Rick, he'd be busy figuring out how to put his heart back together.

"Dad, will you give us a moment alone, please?" Delaney spoke to her father, but her gaze remained fixed on him.

She bore no resemblance to the woman who'd brazenly shed her clothes for him last night. Right now, Delaney appeared every bit the powerful executive, from her sleek navy suit and understated gold bangles, to her all-business pumps.

But then, Rick had always admired that about her. She had a cool, unflappable facade that he now knew hid a passionate, warm-hearted woman inside.

"Of course." Daniel Blair III stood from his spot on the desk and walked toward the door, clapping Rick on the shoulder on his way past while two matching Irish wolfhounds followed their master. "We'll speak later, son."

No sooner had the door closed behind the older man and the dogs than Delaney speared a hand through her thick, dark hair.

"Is that what last night meant to you, Rick? A speed pass out of Atlanta to a team with a better shot at the playoffs?"

Rick had a moment of empathy for the big game animals shot with a tranquilizer gun on those wildlife shows. He halted his forward momentum, stunned still by the accusation.

"Excuse me?" He'd come to the house with every intention of making things right between him and Delaney. He'd never expected this kind of cold reception. "Were you present for the same night of passion as I was? I thought *you* approached *me.*"

"Because I thought you were honorable and upstanding." Her voice caught and he had a glimpse of the anxiety beneath the anger, but she was quick to hide any hint of vulnerability.

Any hint of caring about him.

That hurt.

Without a doubt, Delaney Blair had developed the power to wound him after just one night together.

"Maybe that's because last night you trusted your gut instead of—" he gestured vaguely with one hand "—your father? The media? Whoever is giving you ideas that you know in your heart don't apply to us or what happened."

He wanted to cross the room and touch her, pull her against him and remind her how electric their connection had been and how powerful it could be if they fed it. But what if she was the kind of woman who fled at the first sign of trouble? Maybe her upbringing in this privileged world on a family compound in Buckhead hadn't prepared her for the kinds of challenges his career put him up against all the time.

Although, in truth, the locker room escapade had more far-reaching consequences than the usual media flare-ups.

"Well, excuse me for second-guessing myself when you barge in here demanding a trade to get away from me."

"Didn't you watch the news conference?" He looked around the room and realized the gargantuan home office was like some British country house from the turn of the century. No electronics except for a couple of lamps. "I met with the media this morning and they're going to be swarming you and your dad. Having me around isn't going to help the team."

Geez, just looking around this room and seeing the legacy of the Blair family and the Atlanta Rebels reinforced his decision to leave. Rick had too much respect for the game and for the club to drag the organization through a personal scandal that would distract the players and management alike.

"And that's what it's all about for you, isn't it? Winning." Delaney stepped toward one of the floor-to-ceiling windows overlooking the massive gardens outside the house. Flowers bloomed despite the relentless heat of Georgia in midsummer.

"No. It's about protecting you and playing the game like it's supposed to be played."

He couldn't put his finger on what had changed between them since he left her office last night, but something had made her distant. Was she really that upset at the idea of him leaving? The thought that it would tear her up as much as it was going to tear him up wasn't any great comfort.

He joined her at the window. She leaned on one side of the casing while he rested a shoulder on the other. Daylight streamed between them, but the reality separating them seemed far more murky.

"Forget about me for a minute. I don't understand what you mean about how you play the game." She shook her head. "How do you think it's supposed to be played that's any different than anyone else in the league?"

"For my whole career I've wanted to be a part of a club that makes it to the playoffs as a team. No one-man bands. No big-ticket guys assembled just to win a series. But a group that picks each other up. A team that plays with as much heart as talent, you know? Like the game means something."

For a moment she nodded, as if she understood. But then she frowned.

"So you want to leave Atlanta because this can't be a team like that anymore. You think what happened last night will disrupt the team's harmony?"

"That's a partial concern." He couldn't do that to the other players and he wouldn't do that to the Blair family. "I think this group of guys could have a real shot at a championship season and I'm not going to mess it up for them. And team aside, I don't want to put you in a position where you have to hide out from the media. I know how much you try to avoid the spotlight. And being with me will make that impossible."

It had sounded reasonable on the way over here in

the car. Delaney had been put in an impossible position by the photographs, and no matter how much she said she would take care of the fallout, the media interest had to be much greater than she'd expected.

Nodding, she squeezed her arms more tightly around herself.

"I understand. But for what it's worth, I've dreamed of being a part of a team that worked together, too. No one-man bands where one person made the decisions about what was best for the team without consulting the other."

He could have handled the rebuke if it hadn't been for the thready emotion in her voice. Underlying that buttoned-up executive exterior remained the sweet, shy woman he'd made love to last night. And he'd hurt her without meaning to.

Crap.

Her old man had led Rick to believe Delaney would suffer because of the scandal, and he'd been quick to buy into it since he felt guilty for landing her half-naked on all the sports blogs. Rick had assured himself he was doing the best thing for all parties concerned by getting the hell out of Dodge.

But what if that's not what she wanted at all?

Before he could pull his thoughts together, she planted the barest whisper of a kiss on his cheek.

"Goodbye, Rick."

5

HIS ARMS MUST HAVE SNAKED around her while she was saying goodbye, because when she attempted to walk away, his hands were on her waist, holding her in place.

"You know, on the other hand, sometimes a good scandal really brings a team together." He trotted out a completely unexpected response to her words of parting.

And she might have laughed at the absurdity of the comment if her heart hadn't been breaking. As it stood, she held herself very still so as not to sink into his strong arms all over again and tell him to never let her go.

Although she might have shed her clothes last night, she didn't plan to shed her dignity today, no matter how much of a life-changing event sleeping with the first baseman had turned out to be.

"Well, in that case, I hope the Rebels can recover from this one and still go on to take the championship without you." She didn't say it to hurt him. She really wanted a win for the Rebels who had weathered plenty of personnel changes and "almost but not quite" seasons.

Still, he didn't release her waist.

"I mean it," he continued, his thumbs starting a slow glide on the waist of her short suit jacket. "Now that I think about it, sometimes those teams that pulled together the hardest did so because one of their players had a particularly tough year. They want to win for the catcher who lost his father in the middle of the season, or they want to win because they were the laughingstock of last place the season before."

"You've hardly experienced a death in the family." Although the expiration of her love life after less than twenty-four hours felt like something she'd mourn for a very long time. "You just got caught with a very determined admirer."

"Is that what you are, Delaney?" He pulled her closer and her heart sped up even though she knew his nearness would only make it tougher to walk away in the end. "My admirer? Because I kind of thought we became a lot more last night."

Her heart gave one last surge of indignation at being tossed aside for his baseball career and her public image.

"I did, too, until you slipped out of my office this morning without so much as a goodbye before deciding you wanted to leave town—and me—for good."

"Delaney, if I thought for a second that you wanted to weather the media storm with me—as a team—I would call your father in here right now and demand a new contract for next year."

The seriousness that she loved about him—loved?— yes, the seriousness she utterly loved about him was evident in his claim. He would really do that.

"You wouldn't just be staying because the Rebels have a shot at going all the way?" She had to know the truth. If it hurt, she could deal with it. But she hadn't shed her shyness and her sarong last night to return to hedging her way through life today.

Not when love was on the line.

"I would stay because *we* have a shot at going all the way." He squeezed her tighter. "Me and you."

Now her pulse spiked wildly, her happiness spilling over like shaken champagne in a victorious locker room.

"Then why didn't you tell me that as soon as you walked in here today?" She wrapped her arms around his neck and pulled him to her, desperate for him. For a future she wouldn't delay another second.

"I thought you deserved better than to be pressured into a relationship just to make your father keep me on the team." He kissed her forehead, the soft press of his lips echoing the understanding that flashed across her mind.

"You hoped I would choose you because I wanted you and not because I was backed into a corner." It was noble and selfless, and just exactly the kind of thing the man she loved would do. "While that's really honorable of you, Rick Warren, if you ever scare me into thinking you're leaving again, I'll trade you to the Alaskan team myself."

He winced.

"You realize there's no major league club up there, don't you?

"You can be the first player contracted," she assured him, wondering if it was possible for a woman to glow from the inside out. She just might be the first case ever.

"Well, that's not going to happen, so you don't need to worry about it."

"Does my father know about this plan of yours?" She'd ship her dad off to Alaska, for that matter, if he had attempted to meddle in her love life ever again.

"No." Rick backed her into the cherry wainscoting beside the window, out of sight of the gardeners at work on the flowers. "Although he didn't seem one bit surprised that we spent the night together. I think he knew we've been eyeing each other for a while. I do believe he sees more than he would admit."

She shook her head. "He let me think you might have slept with me to secure a ticket off the team."

He shrugged. "Maybe he wanted to see if you were willing to believe the worst of me. But I'm pretty sure that by the time all the smoke blew over today, he was hoping there'd be a proposal in the works."

She felt the heat crawl up her cheeks. "He is ridiculously old-fashioned."

"Are you kidding? I think that's great. And since I've been watching your every move for the last year and a half, I feel like I know you very well already." Rick reached into his shirt and withdrew a clunky gold band with a tiny diamond in the middle and lots of engraving. "Enough to think a proposal isn't a bad idea."

"Rick!" She wondered if a more sophisticated woman would tell him not to be silly, and that of course she wasn't expecting *marriage* after a single night together. But the look in his eyes told her this was no joke. "I couldn't possibly—"

"How about we call it a pre-engagement ring and let the media make of it what they will?" A rare grin lifted the corner of his mouth. "You and I can sort it all out at our leisure, but in the meantime, I would be honored if you'd wear my college national championship ring from the year we captured the division I title. I figure it's a good place holder until I can find a ring more—"

"You really mean it?" She was shaking like a leaf as he held an irreplaceable piece of jewelry close to her hand like an offering.

"I'm crazy about you, Delaney. I love you and I would like you to think about a future with me."

Maybe her jaw dropped. Or maybe it was the tears that were rolling down her cheeks all of the sudden, but something must have tipped him off that she was completely overwhelmed because he cupped her cheek with infinite tenderness.

"I know this might seem sudden to you, but it's been a long time coming for me. And a wise woman I know taught me life is too short to wait for happiness to find us."

"Oh, Rick!" She clutched his hand, hardly daring to believe her dreams could come true simply by daring to act on them. "I've loved you since your very first line drive to right field that brought in—"

"Dwight Wrigley for the win against Florida." He grinned. "And I've loved you since the first meet and greet after spring training when you took me on a tour of the trophy room without ever once making eye contact."

Laughter burst through the emotions lodged at the base of her throat. "I'm no good at flirting."

His grin turned wolfish. "You sure got my attention when you were ready."

Warmth tingled through her.

"I would be so honored to spend my future with you, Rick Warren." She waggled her fingers at the diamond in his hand. "And I'm proud to wear your ring."

As he slid the piece onto her finger, he bent to brush a kiss along her lips.

Without question, Delaney knew they were sealing a bargain to last a lifetime.

Epilogue

Three months later

"SO HOW DO YOU LIKE the taste of humble pie, big guy?"

Ozzie, the new lead disc jockey on Big Apple Sports Radio grinned as the fax came across the news wire listing the year's Gold Glove winners.

His morning-show partner had gotten demoted from the drive-time show to a late-night slot after ticking off a few too many of the game's fans with inaccurate information and all-around lazy commentary. The program coordinator had given the top spot to Oz, citing his vast baseball knowledge and appeal to listeners.

"He's not the only one shoveling it down," Scott, Oz's new color man, appeared over his shoulder to check out the Gold Glove winners on the list. The kid was sharp and outspoken, but he never took the low road. "If you'd asked me last summer, I probably would have predicted these guys going down in flames."

"Baseball players are young," Ozzie remarked, tearing off the printout in preparation for the 6:00 a.m. show. "And they live every second in the spotlight. You think they're the only guys who make an occasional misstep? But no one predicts we're going down in flames when we mess up."

Oz had never liked the way public figures ended up as punching bags so often, and he hoped his show would be different.

"Brian Marshall went down in flames," Scott observed, picking up the coffeepot for his morning java.

"Watch your step, kid," Oz threatened without any heat. He wasn't sorry to see the loudmouth off the a.m. airwaves, but he kept that opinion to himself. "All I'm saying is that these guys deserve a break. They play more games than any other professional athlete and they work in a highly competitive field."

"Some work harder than others," Scott observed, pointing to the mug shots of the players taking home fielding honors this season. Virtually every player Brian Marshall had pegged as a thug had proved instrumental for his team this season and every last damn one of them had copped the trophy for his respective position.

"It was so damn cool to see Rick Warren lead a team to the World Series." Chalk one up for the old dudes. It had taken Warren a decade, but he'd proven that you didn't have to be a showboat to bring your team to the playoffs.

"Plus, he married Blair's daughter. You know they'll tap him for a coaching slot in another season or two." Scott shook his head, as if to suggest some guys had all the luck.

Oz knew better. The guy had served his time in the trenches. Baseball was fortunate to have him around as a counterpoint to the young studs that focused solely on their batting average. The rookies could learn a thing or two about the game from a guy like Warren.

"You know," Scott continued, glopping cream cheese on his bagel and coating half the printout with what he splattered around. "Now that I think on it, all these guys took up with women this year."

Ozzie thought back to the news bits that had come in over the last few months. "That's right. Montero is still courting the singer."

"I'm in love with Jamie McRae, man," Scott declared. "Let's invite Montero on the show and ask him to bring her along. She can sing that baseball song of hers."

"What are we, *Entertainment Tonight?*" Ozzie swiped off the cream cheese. "We're getting back to serious baseball around here, remember?"

Although Jamie McRae was the bomb.

"Hey, I've got it." Scott snapped his fingers. "We invite Javier Velasquez and Brody Davis on the same show and see if they go at it again."

"Not interested. Besides, it's old news. Those two have been buds since, like, a week after their brawl." Oz had read a feature piece on them a few weeks ago. Apparently their new girlfriends had become fast friends while comparing notes during the playoff games.

"Fine." Scott ripped a paper towel off the roll and swiped the rest of the cream cheese away. "So you're saying we just talk about the news. No theatrics."

"Maybe just this once." Oz clapped his new commentator on the shoulder then made his way toward his seat at the microphone. "You know as well as I do, there'll be a whole new batch of hotheads and heartbreakers next spring to get everyone all fired up again."

"Right." Scott tromped behind him, trailing news printouts and crumbs. "Until then, thank God for football season, right, boss?"

* * * * *

RICK'S APPOINTMENT with his attorney early Wednesday morning went only moderately better than his meeting with social services the day before. The prognosis wasn't great—but at least his attorney was going to file a motion for DNA testing. Just so Rick could petition to see the child…his sister's baby. The sister he didn't know he had until it was too late.

The rest of what his attorney said had been downhill from there.

Cell phone in hand before he'd even reached his Nitro, Rick punched in the speed dial number he'd programmed the day before.

Maybe foster parent Sue Bookman hadn't received his message. Or had lost his number. Maybe she didn't want to talk to him. At this point he didn't much care what she wanted.

"Hello?" She answered before the first ring was complete. And sounded breathless.

Young and breathless.

"Ms. Bookman?"

"Yes. This is Rick Kraynick, right?"

"Yes, ma'am."

"I recognized your number on caller ID," she said, her voice uneven, as though she was still engaged in whatever physical activity had her so breathless to begin with. "I'm sorry I didn't get back to you. I've been a little…distracted."

The words came in more disjointed spurts. Was she jogging?

"No problem," he said, when, in fact, he'd spent the better part of the night before watching his phone. And fretting. "Did I get you at a bad time?"

"No worse than usual," she said, adding, "Better than some. So, how can I help?"

God, if only this could be so easy. He'd ask. She'd help. And life could go well. At least for one little person in his family.

It would be a first.

"Mr. Kraynick?"

"Yes. Sorry. I was…are you sure there isn't a better time to call?"

"I'm bouncing a baby, Mr. Kraynick. It's what I do."

"Is it Carrie?" he asked quickly, his pulse racing.

"How do you know Carrie?" She sounded defensive, which wouldn't do him any good.

"I'm her uncle," he explained, "her mother's— Christy's—older brother, and I know you have her."

"I can neither confirm nor deny your allegations, Mr. Kraynick. Please call social services." She rattled off the number.

"Wait!" he said, unable to hide his urgency. "Please," he said more calmly. "Just hear me out."

"How did you find me?"

"A friend of Christy's."

"I'm sorry I can't help you, Mr. Kraynick," she said softly. "This conversation is over."

"I grew up in foster care," he said, as though that gave him some special privilege. Some insider's edge.

"Then you know you shouldn't be calling me at all."

"Yes… But Carrie is my niece," he said. "I need to see her. To know that she's okay."

"You'll have to go through social services to arrange that."

"I'm sure you know it's not as easy as it sounds. I'm a single man with no real ties and I've no intention of petitioning for custody. They aren't real eager to give me the time of day. I never even knew Carrie's mother. For all intents and purposes, our mother didn't raise either one of us. All I have going for me is half a set of genes. My lawyer's on it, but it could be weeks— months—before this is sorted out. Carrie could be adopted by then. Which would be fine, great for her, but then I'd have lost my chance. I don't want to take her. I won't hurt her. I just have to see her."

"I'm sorry, Mr. Kraynick, but…"

* * * * *

*Find out if Rick Kraynick will ever have a chance
to meet his niece.
Look for A DAUGHTER'S TRUST by
Tara Taylor Quinn,
available in September 2009.*

**We'll be spotlighting a different series
every month throughout 2009
to celebrate our 60th anniversary.**

**Look for Harlequin® Superromance®
in September!**

*Celebrate with
The Diamond Legacy
miniseries!*

Follow the stories of four cousins as they come to terms
with the complications of love and what it means to
be a family. Discover with them the sixty-year-old secret
that rocks not one but two families.

A DAUGHTER'S TRUST by *Tara Taylor Quinn*
September

FOR THE LOVE OF FAMILY by *Kathleen O'Brien*
October

LIKE FATHER, LIKE SON by *Karina Bliss*
November

A MOTHER'S SECRET by *Janice Kay Johnson*
December

Available wherever books are sold.

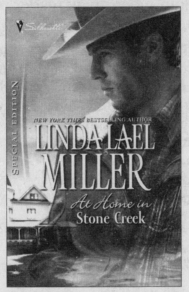

Do you crave dark and sensual paranormal tales?

Get your fix with Silhouette Nocturne!

REQUEST YOUR FREE BOOKS!

2 FREE NOVELS PLUS 2 FREE GIFTS!

HARLEQUIN®

Blaze™

Red-hot reads!

YES! Please send me 2 FREE Harlequin® Blaze™ novels and my 2 FREE gifts (gifts are worth about $10). After receiving them, if I don't wish to receive any more books, I can return the shipping statement marked "cancel". If I don't cancel, I will receive 6 brand-new novels every month and be billed just $4.24 per book in the U.S. or $4.71 per book in Canada. That's a savings of 15% off the cover price. It's quite a bargain. Shipping and handling is just 50¢ per book.* I understand that accepting the 2 free books and gifts places me under no obligation to buy anything. I can always return a shipment and cancel at any time. Even if I never buy another book, the two free books and gifts are mine to keep forever.

151 HDN EYS2   351 HDN EYTE

Name	(PLEASE PRINT)	
Address		Apt. #
City	State/Prov.	Zip/Postal Code

Signature (if under 18, a parent or guardian must sign)

Mail to the **Harlequin Reader Service:**
IN U.S.A.: P.O. Box 1867, Buffalo, NY 14240-1867
IN CANADA: P.O. Box 609, Fort Erie, Ontario L2A 5X3

Not valid to current subscribers of Harlequin Blaze books.

**Want to try two free books from another line?
Call 1-800-873-8635 or visit www.morefreebooks.com.**

* Terms and prices subject to change without notice. Prices do not include applicable taxes. N.Y. residents add applicable sales tax. Canadian residents will be charged applicable provincial taxes and GST. Offer not valid in Quebec. This offer is limited to one order per household. All orders subject to approval. Credit or debit balances in a customer's account(s) may be offset by any other outstanding balance owed by or to the customer. Please allow 4 to 6 weeks for delivery. Offer available while quantities last.

Your Privacy: Harlequin Books is committed to protecting your privacy. Our Privacy Policy is available online at www.eHarlequin.com or upon request from the Reader Service. From time to time we make our lists of customers available to reputable third parties who may have a product or service of interest to you. If you would prefer we not share your name and address, please check here. ☐

HB09R3

COMING NEXT MONTH

Available August 25, 2009

#489 GETTING PHYSICAL Jade Lee

For American student/waitress Zoe Lewis, Tantric sex—sex as a spiritual experience—is a totally foreign concept. Strange, yet irresistible. Then she's partnered with Tantric master Stephen Chiu…and discovers just how far great sex can take a girl!

#490 MADE YOU LOOK Jamie Sobrato
Forbidden Fantasies

She spies with her little eye… From the privacy of her living room Arianna Day has a front-row seat for her neighbor Noah Quinn's sex forays. And she knows he's the perfect man to end her bout of celibacy. Now to come up with the right plan to make him look…

#491 TEXAS HEAT Debbi Rawlins
Encounters

Four college girlfriends arrive at the Sugarloaf ranch to celebrate an engagement announcement. With all the tasty cowboys around, each will have a reunion weekend she'll never forget!

#492 FEELS LIKE THE FIRST TIME Tawny Weber
Dressed to Thrill

Zoe Gaston hated high school. So the thought of going back for her reunion doesn't exactly thrill her. Little does she guess that there's a really hot guy who's been waiting ten long years to do just that!

#493 HER LAST LINE OF DEFENSE Marie Donovan
Uniformly Hot!

Instructing a debutante in survival training is not how Green Beret Luc Boudreau planned to spend his temporary leave. Problem is, he kind of likes this feisty fish out of water and it turns out the feeling's mutual. But will they find any common ground other than their shared bedroll…?

#494 ONE GOOD MAN Alison Kent
American Heroes: The Texas Rangers

Jamie Danby needs a hero—badly. As the only witness to a brutal shooting, she's been flying below the radar for years. Now her cover's blown and she needs a sexy Texas Ranger around 24/7 to make her feel safe. The best sex of her life is just a bonus!